# INDECENT EXPOSURE

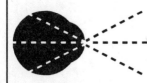

This Large Print Book carries the
Seal of Approval of N.A.V.H.

# INDECENT EXPOSURE

## STUART WOODS

**THORNDIKE PRESS**
*A part of Gale, Cengage Learning*

GALE
CENGAGE Learning·

Farmington Hills, Mich • San Francisco • New York • Waterville, Maine
Meriden, Conn • Mason, Ohio • Chicago

## GALE
CENGAGE Learning·

**LIBRARY OF CONGRESS CATALOGING-IN-PUBLICATION DATA**

Names: Woods, Stuart, author.
Title: Indecent exposure / by Stuart Woods.
Description: Large print edition. | Waterville, Maine : Thorndike Press, a part of Gale, a Cengage Company, 2017. | Series: A Stone Barrington novel ; 42 | Series: Thorndike Press large print basic
Identifiers: LCCN 2017016987 | ISBN 9781432839253 (hardcover) | ISBN 143283925X (hardcover)
Subjects: LCSH: Barrington, Stone (Fictitious character)—Fiction. | Private investigators—Fiction. | Large type books. | BISAC: FICTION / Action & Adventure. | FICTION / Suspense. | FICTION / Thrillers. | GSAFD: Suspense fiction.
Classification: LCC PS3573.O642 I53 2017b | DDC 813/.54—dc23
LC record available at https://lccn.loc.gov/2017016987

Published in 2017 by arrangement with G. P Putnam's Sons, an imprint of Penguin Publishing Group, a division of Penguin Random House LLC

Printed in the United States of America
1 2 3 4 5 6 7 21 20 19 18 17

# Indecent Exposure

# 1

Stone Barrington landed the Citation CJ3 Plus smoothly at Manassas Airport, in Virginia. As he taxied to the FBO he noticed a large black SUV parked on the ramp. To his eye it looked government and armored, and he wondered what VIP could be landing at the small, general aviation airport. His curiosity was soon satisfied: as he parked and cut his engines the vehicle began to move, and it stopped off his wingtip.

Stone ran through his shutdown checklist, then withdrew from the cockpit and opened the cabin door. A man in a blue suit with a shiny button in his lapel stood there.

"Mr. Barrington?"

"Yes," Stone replied, still mystified.

"Secretary Barker asked us to meet you."

Stone then noticed a second, similarly dressed man standing by the SUV and surveying the ramp, and he realized that Holly Barker had been sworn in as secretary of state. It was Election Day, and President Katharine Lee had, apparently, jumped the gun on her appointment, since she was the once and, if things went as they were supposed to, future President.

Stone handed the man a key. "Front luggage compartment," he said. "Take everything."

The car stopped in front of the elegant double-width town house in Georgetown. Stone had not seen the place for some years, but he now owned it, having come to an arrangement with the Lees by which he had exchanged his Santa Fe house, plus an adjoining property and some cash, for this house, which former President Will Lee had owned with his late father since he was an aide to a United States senator.

The driver pressed a button on the sun visor and a garage door opened. The vehicle drove into the basement garage, and the security man opened the door for him. "The elevator is straight ahead," he said. "We'll get your luggage upstairs."

Stone thanked him, got into the elevator, and pressed the G button. A moment later he emerged into the main floor central hallway, where there was a buzz of people and voices. Caterers were arranging the living room for a party, and Holly Barker stood in the center of the room, directing traffic. She saw Stone and ran to him, throwing her arms around his neck. "Here you are!" she sang out in a happy voice.

"Here I am, indeed," he replied, joining her in the hug. As always, she felt just wonderful. "I thought you were expecting just a few friends," he said.

"It got out of hand," she replied. "We're at fifty and counting. I'm learning that nobody declines an invitation from a high cabinet member. The caterers are felling another ox."

"So, you're already a cabinet member?"

"I was sworn in this morning."

"My congratulations," he said, kissing her.

"Come on upstairs, I'll show you your room."

Stone followed her into the elevator and took advantage of their momentary privacy to kiss her and pull her closer with his hand on her ass. They broke before the door opened.

She led him into what was, obviously, the master bedroom, which had two dressing rooms and two baths. "By tomorrow, all of Washington will know we're sharing a bed," she said. "I talked it over with Kate, and we agreed that it was better not to bother with a nod to convention, just to go ahead and let the world get used to the idea of a single woman with a sex life as a cabinet secretary — no fuss, no bother."

"I'm fine with that," Stone said. "It will do wonders for my reputation."

"Your bags are in that dressing room." She pointed. "You get unpacked, and by the way, we've upgraded to black tie. I knew you would bring a dinner jacket."

"You know me too well. What time do we make an appearance downstairs?"

"Seven o'clock," she replied. "I've rented three big-screen TVs, and that's when the action begins. Would you like a drink now?"

"I'd like a nap now, if that's all right. I was out with Dino and Viv until late last night. They were sorry they couldn't come, but the mayor stole them for his party."

"Apparently, my social magnet doesn't reach as far as New York," she said.

"It does, it just can't compete with the mayor's social magnet."

"I'll wake you at six," she said, pushing him onto the bed and pulling off his shoes. She threw a light blanket over him and kissed him on the forehead.

Stone sank into the soft bed and closed his eyes.

At six, Holly, already half-dressed, woke

him, and he shaved and showered and got into his dinner suit. At five minutes before seven, they got on the elevator.

"You are gorgeous," he said, looking her up and down.

"I'm afraid I've infringed on your generosity for a whole new wardrobe," she said. "The new job requires a lot more dressing up than national security advisor to the President. Your credit card is smoking."

"That's what it's for," Stone replied. "Keep the credit card and use it as you will."

The door opened, and they spilled into the hallway. There were already many voices coming from the living room.

The first person Stone recognized was Senator Saltonstall of New York. They shook hands warmly. "Stone, may I introduce my daughter Celeste, and her beau, Peter Rule?"

It was the first time Stone had met Kate Lee's son by her first marriage. He was a handsome young man of around thirty, and Ms. Saltonstall was a genuine beauty. "I'm delighted you're here," Stone said to Peter. "Your mother has told me about you."

"Uh-oh," Peter said. "I hope she hasn't blown our secret."

"She has not," Stone replied, "but I think you just did."

"He has a big mouth," Celeste said, kissing him on the cheek, thereby displaying her left hand, revealing about eight carats of glittering, emerald-cut stone.

"And you have a big diamond," Stone said, "so it must not be too much of a secret."

"Dad wants to announce it tonight," Celeste said, "before we adjourn to the White House for the latter part of the evening. Mom and Will have to touch a few bases, including campaign headquarters."

Stone knew from his mother that Peter was planning a run for New York's other senatorial seat at the midterm. Stone leaned forward and whispered into Celeste's ear, "You'd better get something smaller for campaigning."

"I hadn't thought of that," she said, "but you're right."

Holly pulled him away and began introducing him to all the others, a few of whom he'd met before. Then the TV sets were fired up, everybody got some dinner from the buffet, and the evening began.

Everyone was cheerful and happy, looking forward to Kate's second term.

# 2

It was after midnight, and the polls were now closed in the continental USA. The crowd was lighter by half and what little conversation there was was subdued. Everyone was glued to the TVs.

Kate had gone into the election with a nine-point lead in the polls and was predicted to get more than 400 electoral votes. Instead, she was struggling toward 270. That morning's newspapers had headlined a story that Will Lee had taken a fifty-million-dollar bribe from a Saudi prince, to get a huge arms deal with the USA. The Lee campaign had flooded the airwaves with her surrogates, denying everything and blaming the lie on her opponent. From what Stone could see on the TV screens, especially the jubilant reporting on Fox News, Kate's campaign had taken on water, and with very little time to right the ship.

Holly stared at the screen. "I'm going to

be the shortest-serving secretary of state in history."

"It's going to come down to Florida," Stone said. "How is Kate feeling about Florida?"

"Just great, until today," Holly replied.

A waiter passed among them with a frosty champagne bottle, topping off glasses.

An anchorman came back from commercial, holding a sheet of paper in one hand and a microphone in the other.

"Here it comes," Holly said.

"Some incredible news has just come in," the man said. "Let's go to Cassie Crane outside Republican campaign headquarters in New York."

A young woman with a microphone stood on the sidewalk in a light rain, next to a geeky young man wearing a dark suit and heavy glasses. "Chris, I'm here with Jason Foxworthy, who is a poll analyst with the Jack Marion campaign. Jason, I think it's best for you to tell your own story, then we'll have some questions."

"Thank you, Cassie," the young man said in a surprisingly deep voice. "Late last night I picked up a phone in our office and overheard a conversation between James Heckley, a speechwriter for Senator Marion, and Max Wafford, the owner of the *Washing-*

*ton Debater,* a conservative newspaper. I know it was Heckley because I could see him across the room as he spoke, and I recognized Wafford's voice from seeing him on TV shows. Also, Heckley called him Max, twice, during the conversation. They were confirming details of the big story that broke today about the alleged bribe taken by Will Lee. In fact, it might be more accurate to say that they were getting their stories straight, because Heckley was reading a draft of the story, and Wafford was suggesting changes to make it stronger and more damning. When they had finished their conversation, Wafford said that he was holding the *Debater*'s presses to get it into the early-morning edition. They both seemed very pleased with themselves."

"Let's be clear, Jason," Cassie said. "You are saying that you overheard James Heckley and Max Wafford contriving this story?"

"That's exactly what I'm saying," Foxworthy replied. "The story is a lie, a complete fabrication." He held up an iPhone. "And I recorded all but ten or fifteen seconds of their phone conversation." He held up a wrinkled sheet of paper. "And I retrieved the draft from the wastebasket beside James Heckley's desk."

Cassie addressed the camera. "Chris, I

15

have to get Jason to a secure location right away, and we've got a car standing by for him. There's one more revelation in the story, though — I've heard from two campaign staffers that James Heckley left campaign headquarters nearly two hours ago for Teterboro Airport, where a private jet was waiting to fly him out of New York. First reports say that the airplane had filed a flight plan for Caracas, Venezuela, but of course that destination could be changed en route. Back to you, Chris."

The anchor stared gravely into the camera. "Cassie, that was a brilliant piece of reportage, and we here all thank you for it. Unfortunately, the polls have already closed."

It was as though lightning had struck the living room — everyone was talking at once, some happy, others in tears. Two people were shouting into their cell phones.

Stone stood up and pointed at the TV set. "Everybody shut up!" he shouted.

The anchorman was now standing next to the campaign map. "We have just heard that Florida has reported its election results, and by a margin of less than four thousand votes, Katharine Lee has carried the state, and with Florida's twenty-nine electoral votes, has been reelected President of the

United States, winning three hundred and three electoral votes. I think it's fair to say that a national catastrophe has been averted."

Cheering erupted in the room, and Holly fell into Stone's arms.

Stone awoke a little after seven am to the sound of Holly talking on the phone. She hung up. "Big news," she said. "Max Wafford has been arrested by the FBI on a charge of election tampering. They're still looking for James Heckley, but his flight diverted to Mexico City and landed there early this morning."

Stone switched on the TV, and every news station was reporting its version of the Heckley/Wafford story. Kate's victory in the election seemed almost like an afterthought. He switched it off. "I don't think I can take this on an empty stomach."

As if on cue, a maid knocked and pushed a cart into the room. Moments later, Stone and Holly were sitting up in bed eating scrambled eggs and bacon. The TV was back on.

"And what does your day hold?" Stone asked.

"I'm visiting the State Department and being introduced to my staff, or at least, those I don't already know from working with them on the National Security Council. Stan Adamson is going to be there to introduce me. And you?"

"I'm due for a drink with Kate and Will in the family quarters at six. So are you."

"Oh, yes."

"Since they appointed me their personal attorney, I've put together a team at Woodman & Weld, which will be known as The Barrington Group. There's a thick envelope on the table across the room containing a document I put together explaining everything. I'll deliver a copy to them this evening."

"I'll look forward to reading it."

"There's something else I want to discuss with you, but I don't want to talk about it here." He tapped an ear with his forefinger.

Holly looked shocked. "Really? Not here?"

"That's correct," Stone said. "We'll talk about it later, when the circumstances are more favorable."

"Whatever you say," Holly replied. She jumped out of bed. "I've got to get myself together."

# 3

That evening they took the elevator to the basement garage, where Holly's SUV awaited them. The street door was open, and Stone pulled her up the ramp with him.

"I'll be just a minute," Holly called to her security team.

Stone put his briefcase into the SUV, then they turned down the block.

"Okay, shoot," Holly said, taking Stone's arm.

Stone didn't hesitate. "I want you to have the house swept by your security team for listening devices, and I want them to do this at least every three or four days, but not on a regular schedule. Your car, too."

"Are you coming over all paranoid on me, Stone?"

"I don't think that the political opposition is going to cheerfully accept the election results," he said, "and we've already seen how far they're willing to go."

"But Wafford is already in jail, and Heckley is a fugitive."

"Wafford has certainly already been bailed out, and being a fugitive won't keep Heckley from operating for long. Even if I'm wrong about this, it won't hurt to be a little paranoid."

"All right, whatever you say."

"Also, you have to start being more careful in how you proceed with your life."

"What do you mean?"

"For instance, you had your car meet me at the Manassas Airport yesterday. That's personal use of an official vehicle, and that could come back to bite you on the ass."

"I suppose," Holly said.

"When you get to the office tomorrow, I want you to report that to your chief administrative officer, have him give you a bill for the cost of that service, and reimburse the State Department with a personal check. Thereafter, anytime you make personal use of any government property or service, do the same thing. You want to establish a consistent paper trail."

"Oh, all right."

They reached the next corner, and Stone turned them back toward the house. "The other thing is, we're probably being photographed while we're on this little stroll, so you'd better get ready to see the photographs in the *National Inquisitor,* because that little rag is one of Max Wafford's properties."

"I told you, I've already discussed this with Kate, and she's fine with me being a single woman with a sex life."

"Tomorrow morning I want you to meet with your public affairs officer at State and discuss me with him or her."

"Her."

"Have her prepare a few statements to the press, to be distributed as soon as such an article runs. We'll be mentioned in the more prestigious papers, too — you can count on that, so be ready for an instant response."

"Okay."

"And don't mention a sex life — make it a personal life. They won't need any help from you in bringing sex into the story."

"Well, they won't be able to suggest I'm a lesbian."

"No, they'll probably hint that you're bisexual. Don't let yourself be photographed hugging or kissing a woman. And, apart from the statements that you and your public affairs officer are going to write, don't make any statements or answer any questions on your personal life. You'll want

21

to establish that rule immediately and stick to it."

"All right. Anything else?"

"Yes. Do you recall an occasion in your personal life, many years back, when you were chief of police at Orchid Beach, when you liberated a suitcase full of cash before, during, or after a major drug bust?"

"I seem to recall such an incident," Holly said.

"And you may recall opening a numbered account in a Cayman Islands bank, which issued you a credit card for your surreptitious use."

"Yes."

"I've given a great deal of thought as to how you might legitimize these funds, which now amount to, what, seven million dollars?"

"Eight and a half."

"I've come to the conclusion that any action we might take with regard to laundering that money would be far too dangerous to contemplate, so you must immediately stop drawing on those funds with your credit card or depositing or withdrawing further funds. Do you have a legitimate investment account?"

"Yes, with a brokerage house."

"Good. For as long as you're secretary of

state, and maybe for some time after that, don't go near any of the Cayman funds."

Holly nodded. "You're right."

"And avoid any trips — official or un-official — to the Cayman Islands. When you opened the account, was your passport stamped on entering that country?"

"No. I'm not that stupid."

"You're going to be issued a diplomatic passport, so shred your old one and lock your credit card in your safe at home." He paused. "On second thought, give the card to me, and I'll secure it."

"All right, I'll give it to you tonight."

"And I hope I don't have to tell you not to use a personal e-mail server?"

Holly laughed. "Of course not."

"And close any personal e-mail accounts you already have. Have you usually done your personal e-mail on your own com-puter?"

"Yes, it's at home."

"Then remove the hard drive from it and give it to me, along with your credit card, and install a new hard drive."

"I know how to do that."

"The State Department will issue you a new phone, perhaps more than one. Give me the old one and buy a new iPhone for strictly personal use, as in e-mails to your father and his wife or to me. Even then, be very circumspect about what you say in any e-mail and use that phone as little as possible."

"Why not just destroy the old hard drive and the phone?"

"Because you may find yourself in circumstances where it's to your advantage to turn over old devices. That way, no one can say you've destroyed them to hide something."

"I see."

"You're also going to have to be circumspect in your personal life, especially with what invitations you accept, even to dinner parties. In those cases, always ask your hostess to send you a guest list. You don't want to find yourself backed into a corner by a journalist who demands some background or a quote."

"Can I see men other than you?" she asked slyly.

"Of course not!"

"I thought not."

"Oh, all right, but before you make any dates, ask your people to run a background check on the men."

"You're serious?"

"Do you want to find out later that somebody you've slept with is an unregistered lobbyist for some creepy foreign regime? Or that he has two wives and families in different cities?"

Holly sighed. "You know what I'm really happy about?" she asked.

"What?"

"I'm just delighted that I don't have an ex-husband out there, spreading lies about me, or even worse, the truth!"

Laughing, they got into the car and left for the White House.

# 4

They drove through the main gate of the White House and were met by two men, one who parked the car, the other who escorted them upstairs to the family quarters.

The Lees greeted them with hugs, handshakes, and kisses, and so did Kate's son Peter Rule, and his fiancée, Celeste Saltonstall.

"Would you like a drink?" Kate asked them. A White House butler stood by to take the order.

"Yes, but first we have some business to conduct," Stone said. "I'll be as brief as possible."

Everyone took a seat, and Stone placed his briefcase on the coffee table and opened it. "Presidents Lee, have you any objection to Holly, Peter, and Celeste being present during this meeting?"

"None," the two said simultaneously.

"We're going to need a notary standing by to authenticate your signatures."

"We're ahead of you on that," Will said. "There's one waiting outside in the hallway." A Secret Service agent, who had been standing inside the outer door, discreetly stepped out into the hall and closed the door behind him, and the butler vanished.

Stone removed three handsomely leather-bound, thick folders from his briefcase and handed them to Will, Kate, and Holly, whose names were embossed on the covers.

"I would like to make a recording of these proceedings," Stone said, "for both accuracy and historical purposes. Have I your permission?"

"Yes," they all said.

He set a recorder on the coffee table and switched it on. "If you will open your folders, the first document you see will be a letter appointing my firm and me as your personal attorneys. You have seen this before, and no changes have been requested since then. If you are agreeable, please sign the document. My signature is already present, representing the firm."

Everybody signed.

"Now, we have set up a sort of mini law firm inside the larger firm, to be called The Barrington Group at Woodman & Weld. The members of the group are four partners, including me, four associates, and eight assistants. The second in command, as it were, is Herbert Fisher, who speaks for me in my absence. Their photographs and biographies are in your folders, along with all their contact information — phones, faxes, e-mail, et cetera. At some point when you're in New York, drop by and be introduced to all of them. They are all available to you twenty-four/seven, and all of them will be briefed on all the client information, so that any one of them can help you. As you know, I live in more than one place, but in my physical absence, I am always available by cell phone and e-mail."

Everybody leafed through the sheets.

"Currently eight clients are served by the group, the Presidents Lee, Secretary Barker, and five of my existing clients — Strategic Services, the Steele Insurance Group, the Arrington Hotel Group, Laurence Hayward, a private client, and Triangle Partnership, a new investment group set up by myself and two others, Michael Freeman of Strategic Services and Charles Fox, formerly of Goldman Sachs, who is our chief investment officer. Charley Fox will always be available if, in addition to your brokers, you require another opinion concerning the purchase or sale of an investment. Over the next few years the partnership will be conducting IPOs from our existing holdings, and you may have the opportunity to invest in those on favorable terms, after consulting your own financial advisors.

"All the personal files you have given us have been digitized and are available to all those in the group, and the originals will be stored in a separate, secure area of Woodman & Weld's storage facility. The group has its own local area network, and stringent security measures are already in effect.

"Next in your folders are the wills and trusts we have drawn up for you, and your living wills, each incorporating any changes you may have asked for. Please sign these where indicated, and we will need the notary and three other witnesses to sign, as well."

The notary, two agents, and the butler were called in to witness the documents, then departed.

Stone removed copies of another document and gave them to Kate. "This is a deed of gift of your former Georgetown residence from my ownership to that of the State Department, for the purpose of housing secretaries of state. You have already approved the terms and conditions." Stone closed his briefcase. "And that concludes our business, unless you have further questions or requests."

No one said anything for a moment, then Peter Rule cleared his throat. "Stone, I would like to retain you and your group as my personal attorneys, if that is agreeable to you."

"Of course, Peter," Stone said. "Let's meet when you're next in New York to discuss that in detail."

"And, of course, when Celeste and I are married, she would also like to retain your services."

"I'd be delighted. Anything else?"

No one spoke.

"In that case, I'd like to extend an invitation to you all. I am a partner in the ownership of a recently completed yacht of a hundred and twenty-five feet, with seven guest cabins, and I'd like to invite you on a cruise during the holiday season, dates to be agreed later. The yacht will be based in Fort Lauderdale for the winter, but we can all meet it at any convenient port. Presidents Lee, you should know that there is a helicopter landing pad aboard, should you wish to arrive with extra discretion, and there is room aboard for two Secret Service agents.

I would expect that the remainder of your detail would travel in an escort vessel of the Navy or Coast Guard."

"We accept!" Kate Lee cried, and the others echoed her.

"Wonderful!" Stone said. "Please consult with each other and let me know your dates, and I will make all the arrangements."

"Time for a drink," Will said.

"Not just yet — first, I have a little surprise for you."

"I'm getting pretty thirsty," Will said.

"Restrain yourself, you'll be happy you did." Stone produced another document from his briefcase. "I have here an offer for each of you from an important New York publisher, with whom I have negotiated terms, which I commend to you. Holly, your offer is for an advance of five million dollars for a work of autobiography, to be completed within two years of your leaving office. The initial payment is one million dollars, on signing." He handed her the offer. "Of course, as a public official, you may not accept this offer until you leave government service, so I will keep it on file for you.

"Kate, your offer is for three works of autobiography for twenty-five million each, and your check is for fifteen million, less commission comprised of the initial payment for each, the remainder to be paid on a schedule to be negotiated. Like Holly, you may not accept until you leave office, and I will keep the offer on file for you.

"Will, your offer is for three works of autobiography, the first of which you have already completed and which the publisher has accepted. The advance for each book is twenty million, and since your manuscript has been accepted, and since you are no longer in public service, I give you a check for thirty million, less our commission, the check being comprised of the entire contract sum for the first volume, and two payments of five million each as the initial payments for the next two books, the remainder to be paid on a schedule to be negotiated." He handed Will the check.

Will clapped his hands, and the butler appeared. "Rex, please locate the best magnum of champagne in the White House cellars and serve it!"

"First, Will," Stone said, "you should sign the offer."

Will did.

Stone tucked the documents into his briefcase. "And don't forget to pay your taxes," he said, accepting a glass of champagne.

The following morning the maid wheeled in the breakfast cart and handed Stone the papers.

He glanced at the *Washington Debater* and winced. "Now it starts," he said to Holly, handing her the paper, which featured a large front-page photograph, above the fold, of the two of them, arm in arm, during the previous evening's stroll. The headline read:

## NEW SECRETARY OF STATE AND LOVER NEAR GEORGETOWN NEST

Holly looked at the paper. "Oh, God," she said.

# 5

Holly came back from her dressing room, ready for work. Stone was still in bed, reading the papers.

"I've gotta run," she said. "Do you want to come over this afternoon and see my splendid new offices?"

"I'd love to," Stone replied, "but you'll be far too busy for that, and I have to get back to New York."

"That's terrible."

"I know, but you can come and see me."

"Don't count on it until after the inauguration," she said. "I should have everything in better shape after that." Her cell phone rang. "Hello? . . . Good morning, I'm just leaving the house. . . . Oh, yes, I saw it. I'm canceling my subscription to the *Debater* — I didn't even know I had one. We'll deal with it when I get there. Goodbye." She hung up. "That was my public affairs officer, warning me of my new tabloid fame."

She kissed him.

"Take it easy."

"You, too, and if the phone rings, don't answer it. If I need to reach you I'll call you on your cell."

"Got it." They kissed, and she departed.

Stone landed the Citation at Teterboro Airport shortly before noon, and his man, Fred, was there with the car to greet him. Stone locked down the airplane and gave the engine and pitot covers to the lineman to be installed, then got into the car. There was a stack of newspapers on the seat next to him.

"Some reading matter for you, sir," Fred said.

"Oh, thanks." Two tabloids with the same photo he'd seen in the *Debater.* "I didn't know you frequented supermarkets, Fred."

"Helene does." Helene was Stone's Greek housekeeper and cook and Fred's companion. "Joan has been fielding phone calls on that subject all morning."

"Swell," Stone replied, and picked up the *Times,* trusting that he would not see his photograph in those pages. He was wrong. The headline read:

And his photograph was there among the others. The first was: "Holly Barker, formerly national security advisor, has been sworn in as the new secretary of state."

The next to last, with a pretty good photograph, was: "President Lee and the First Gentleman have appointed Stone Barrington, a New York attorney with the firm of Woodman & Weld, as their personal attorney, upon the retirement of his predecessor." He should have anticipated that, but he had not.

Fred garaged the car and took Stone's luggage upstairs while he went to his office.

"Good morning, superstar," Joan sang out.

"Don't start."

"What, has this newfound fame gone to your head?"

"It may be newfound, but it had better not be fame — I'm not up for that."

"I think that henceforth, when your name is mentioned, it will include not only 'New York attorney' but 'paramour of the secretary of state.' "

He emptied his briefcase and handed the

contents to her. "Scan these into the appropriate folders, please, and label the tape with the Lee names and lock it away."

"Certainly. Oh, I almost forgot, here are your phone messages." She handed him a thick envelope.

Stone sat down at his desk and opened the envelope. All the messages but one were from various media sources. The other one was from Dino Bacchetti, his old partner from when he was a cop; Dino was now police commissioner. He handed Joan the media's messages. "Handle these, and don't put any of them through in the future." He called Dino.

"Bacchetti."

"Good morning," Stone said.

"Ah, the secretary of state's new hunk."

"Don't start."

"And how is Holly?"

"Diplomatic."

"And the Lees?"

"Presidential."

"Anything new down there?"

"I met Kate's son from her first marriage, Peter."

"I don't think I knew about him."

"Fathered by Simon Rule, formerly CIA bigwig, now deceased."

"That's convenient. What's the kid like?"

"Rich, from his father's estate, sort of a sandy-haired version of JFK Junior. He's just gotten engaged to Senator Saltonstall's daughter, Celeste. I think he's been flying under the radar so far, but sometime soon you'll start seeing his name in the paper, probably in conjunction with wedding bells."

"Sounds like he has political aspirations."

"If you were the only American ever who had two presidents for parents — or step-parent, in Will's case — wouldn't you have political aspirations?"

"I suppose it would be a waste of genetic material not to. Is he running for something in particular?"

"Junior senator from New York in the half-term elections. I expect him to be well financed."

"Yeah, the one percent will be falling all over him."

"He's been working for Saltonstall for the last four years. Holly says he's had face time with every elected official in New York State, from the governor right down to dogcatcher level, and most of them owe him favors."

"His mother's son."

"You know it."

"You free for dinner tonight? Just you and me — Viv's traveling on business, as usual."

"I'll think of an excuse to be available."

"Patroon at seven?"

"Done."

As he hung up the phone, it rang.

"Yes?"

Joan's voice was a hoarse whisper. "There's a lady here from *Just Folks* magazine." There was awe in her voice.

"Tell her I'm in a meeting until early next year."

"That's not going to work, she caught a glimpse of you through your open door before I could body block her."

"Okay, send her in and I'll boot her out myself."

"Her name is Gloria Parsons."

"Sounds familiar."

"She gets around. Here she comes. Ms. Parsons, Mr. Barrington can see you for just a minute."

Before Stone could hang up the phone a woman stood in his doorway.

"Good afternoon, Mr. Barrington, I'm Gloria Parsons."

Stone reckoned she was six feet tall in her bare feet — not to mention slim, beautifully dressed, high-breasted, and toothy. "Good afternoon," he said. "I'm afraid I don't have much time at the . . ." But she was seated on his sofa before he could finish the sentence, ". . . moment."

"Why don't you just talk to me, instead of returning all those phone calls you got this morning?"

"How'd you . . ."

"Three of them were from me."

". . . know?"

"Look at it this way — give *Just Folks* an exclusive interview, and then you can wave off all the others by telling them that."

She had already produced a pad and a gold pen. "Let's get some basics," she said.

Stone took a chair next to the sofa. "If you're any good, you've already got the basics," he said.

She rewarded him with a big smile. "You know me too well."

# 6

Stone gave her the sixty-second bio. "Born NYC, you figure out when. Attended PS Six, NYU, and NYU law school. A cop for a number of years, most of them as a homicide detective, then of counsel to Woodman & Weld, more recently a partner. Is that basic enough?"

"That's the stuff I've got. Now let's be more thorough. Father was . . ."

"Started as a neighborhood handyman in the Village, went on to become a brilliant carpenter and cabinetmaker and designer and builder of fine furniture."

"For example?"

"My desk," he said, jerking a thumb over his shoulder, "and everything on the floor above, along with other pieces."

"Did he leave you the house?"

"No, that was a great-aunt. She had hired my father to design and build the interior."

"Father's first name?"

"Malon."

"Mother's maiden name?"

"Matilda Stone."

Parsons wrinkled her brow, no doubt fighting Botox. "Sounds familiar."

"Painter."

"Gotcha. She's got some stuff in the American Collection at the Metropolitan, right?"

"Right."

"When and how did you meet Holly Barker?"

"Oh, twelve, fifteen years ago, I guess."

"How?"

"I was in Vero Beach, Florida, to pick up a new airplane at the factory, and I went to a bank to get a cashier's check. While I was standing in line, three or four men with masks and shotguns entered the bank. The guy behind me argued with them and got a load of buckshot in the chest for his trouble. I dialed nine-one-one and did what I could for him until the EMTs arrived, but he didn't make it."

"What has all that to do with Holly Barker?"

"The shooting victim was her fiancé. They were to be married the following day."

"Oh, God."

"Holly was the chief of police in the next

town, Orchid Beach. She looked me up to thank me for trying to help her man, and we kept in touch after that."

"I recall that she joined the CIA not long after that. It seems an odd transition."

"I believe she was of great help to them in breaking up an important drug ring, who were shipping it in from South America. They were impressed with her, as has been everyone who has ever met her."

"How did she hook up with the President?"

"Katharine Rule was a deputy director of the Agency at the time, and Holly distinguished herself, partly under Ms. Rule's tutelage."

"And when did you renew Ms. Barker's acquaintance?"

"She was CIA station chief in New York for some years. I was conveniently located."

"Do you see a lot of her now?"

"Not very much. Since moving to the White House and thence to the State Department, she's been extremely busy."

"And how did you come to the attention of the Lees?"

"Holly introduced us, and I was of help to them on something or other."

"Care to discuss 'something or other'?"

"No. I'll plead attorney-client confidentiality."

"I hate that," Parsons said.

"All journalists do."

Parsons flipped through her shorthand. "Let's see — why did you leave the NYPD?"

"A bullet to the knee. I was invalided out."

"Brave man!"

"There's nothing brave about getting shot. You don't volunteer."

"Why did you get shot?"

"Bad luck."

"Did you shoot the shooter?"

"Tried and missed. My partner put two in him. He was a better shot than I."

"Modest, too."

"Nothing modest about being a not-so-hot shot."

"Why did the Lees choose you as their attorney?"

"Their attorney retired."

"But why did they choose you, in particular?"

"Probably because they knew I wouldn't answer questions like that."

"Touché."

"Il n'y a pas de quoi."

"You speak French?"

"Schoolboy French — I can ask most

44

questions, but I can't understand the answers."

She laughed, a very nice sound. "Same here."

"I'm glad we have something in common." He was, too.

"Will being the presidents' attorney require you to be in Washington a lot?"

"No, the phones still work between here and there."

"So you won't have many opportunities to see Secretary Barker?"

"True."

"And whose company do you keep in New York?"

Stone shrugged. "Whoever will go out with me."

She laughed again. "You mean there are women who won't?"

"In my experience, women are very discerning."

She capped her pen. "May I see some of your father's work?"

"Of course." He took her to the floor above and showed her the living room, dining room, and study.

She was impressed. "He designed and built all of this? The furniture, too?"

"All of it."

"You come from very artistic forebears."

"It's important in life to choose the right parents."

"Do you have artistic sensibilities?"

"Yes, but without the talent. I appreciate the work of others."

She looked at his mother's paintings. "She was very good, wasn't she?"

"She was."

"How many of her works do you have?"

"About a dozen. She left me four, and I've collected the others over the years."

"Well, I won't take any more of your time."

"May we go off the record?"

"If you insist."

"I insist. Are you free for dinner this evening?"

"I am. Where and when?"

"Patroon at seven?"

"Good."

"A friend will be joining us."

"Not another woman."

"A male friend, he'll enjoy you."

"I'll look forward to it."

"I as well." He showed her to the front door.

# 7

As Stone approached Patroon, a cab drove up and Gloria Parsons got out. "Good timing," he said.

"I try."

He showed her into the restaurant; they shed their coats and joined Dino, who was half a drink ahead of them.

"Well, good evening," Dino said, rising as far as the banquette would allow.

"Dino, this is Gloria Parsons. Gloria, Dino Bacchetti. She's for me, Dino, not you."

"It's always that way," Dino said.

"He's married," Stone came back.

"And a good thing, too," Gloria said, "or I'd be with him."

"Good girl!" Dino cried.

"Gloria, what would you like to drink?"

"Whatever you're having."

"You like bourbon?"

"Yuck."

"Then name something, and let's avoid

accidents."

"Belvedere vodka on the rocks, wedge of lime."

A waiter arrived in time to hear that, and he was back in a flash.

"So, you're drinking bourbon?" she asked.

"Almost always."

"What kind?"

"Knob Creek."

"Isn't that two hundred dollars a bottle?"

"That's the limited edition, fourteen years old. I stick with the nine-year-old stuff. I must think of my liver."

"Not too often, I hope."

"Nope."

"Is this guy sitting next to me the commissioner of police?"

"He is, but we don't know how that happened."

"Political influence," Dino said.

"The mayor thinks he's a demigod."

"Then I need his advice."

"Are you planning to get arrested?"

"No, but I know somebody who has been," she said. "He's just arrived at Fishkill, doing three to five for somebody else's real estate scam."

"Ah, an innocent man!" Dino said. "He'll be right at home. Fishkill's full of 'em."

"Do you have any advice for him?"

"Sure, stay out of fights and don't bend over in the shower."

"What could be simpler?" Stone asked.

"My friend's on the delicate side," she said.

"Fishkill's full of delicates," Dino said. "They stay busy, and the time flies."

"Why is he doing all that time?" Stone asked. "Doesn't he know how to bribe a judge? That's what I advise all my clients to do."

"You two are useless," Gloria said. "I think I'm going to need another drink."

"There's a lot of that going around," Dino said, raising a thumb to a waiter.

"Tell Dino what you do, Gloria," Stone said.

"I'm a senior writer at *Just Folks* magazine."

"And why would you have the slightest interest in our Stone?"

"He got his name in the *Times* today."

"Stone, have you been arrested again?"

"No, I'm only a person of interest — tell your guys to stop wasting their time."

Stone looked up to see Laurence and Theresa Hayward enter the restaurant, and they stopped by his table; he introduced them to Gloria.

"Those friends of yours are coming to see

my apartment tomorrow," Laurence said. "I hope they like it. Theresa thinks it's too big for us."

"I hope they like it, too," Stone replied. They said goodbye and went to their table.

"Now, that's interesting," Gloria said.

"What's interesting?" Stone asked.

"You think I don't know who Laurence Hayward is?"

"So?"

"He's the guy who won the all-time biggest Powerball, he has one of the most spectacular apartments in the city, and he's showing it to friends of *yours*. *That's* what's interesting."

Stone pretended to be baffled. "I can't imagine why — *Just Folks* looks at apartments all the time in this city."

"May I hazard a guess at who your friends are?"

"You may not. Do you remember that at the end of our meeting this afternoon I went off the record?"

"Yes, but . . ."

"I haven't gone back on the record, have I?"

"No, but . . ."

"Then we're still off the record."

"Okay, off the record, who are your apartment-hunting friends?"

50

"That's a lovely outfit you're wearing," Stone said. "Who designed it?"

"Don't change the subject."

"I'll change the subject if I like. Who designed your underwear?"

"There, you changed the subject again."

"And I'll keep on doing so until you stop asking annoying questions to which you will not get an answer."

"Listen, I can put two and two together."

"Do you know the difference between a moron and a neurotic?"

"No."

"A moron thinks two and two are five. A neurotic knows two and two are four but it makes him nervous."

She laughed. "There you go changing the subject again."

"It was you who brought up arithmetic."

"You are an exhausting man."

"Then why aren't you exhausted?"

"Okay, I surrender."

"I was going to wait until after dinner to ask you to surrender, but if you're impatient . . ."

She turned to Dino. "Is he always like this?"

"No, he's usually much worse, but wait until he's had another drink."

"Waiter, another drink," Stone said, and

the man came running. "Never mind the drink, just some menus, please."

"What's good here?" Gloria asked.

"What interests you?" Stone asked.

"The beef."

"That's good. Want to share a Chateaubriand?"

"Why not?"

"I can't think of a reason."

They ordered.

# 8

Dino offered them a ride uptown in his official SUV.

"Does it have a siren?" Gloria asked.

"You bet your sweet ass," Dino replied.

"Thank you. May we turn it on?"

"Nope, we might get arrested."

"I should have thought we were immune to that," she said.

"The only time I've turned it on for a civilian was when Stone and I were at dinner and he got a phone call telling him that he had to be in Rome for a board meeting the following morning, and he had fifty minutes to get the last plane at JFK."

"It worked, too," Stone said. "I made the plane and the meeting."

"Now I'm hurt," Gloria said. "You'd turn it on for Stone, but not for me?"

"Do you have a plane to catch?"

"Usually, but not now."

"Not good enough."

"Dino, you are as exasperating as your friend Stone."

"I hope I'm more exasperating than that."

Stone tapped her on the shoulder. "We're almost at my house. Would you like to surrender?"

"I haven't decided yet."

"Then come in for a drink, and we'll discuss it."

"Okay."

The car stopped in front of Stone's house; they thanked Dino and got out.

Stone let them in and took her to the elevator.

"Where are we going?" Gloria asked.

Stone pressed the button. "Up."

"Are there any other choices?"

"Down, but there are no lights on down there." The elevator stopped, and Stone led her toward the master suite.

"Now where are we going?" she asked.

"Down the garden path," he replied, showing her in.

He stopped, faced her, and kissed her lightly.

"What did you have in mind?" she asked.

"Take a big step forward," he replied.

She did so, bringing her pelvis against his.

"Does that answer your question?"

"I suppose it does," she said, kissing him

and pressing herself against his crotch. "Emphatically."

"Would you like me to undress you, or would you rather self-strip?"

"I think I'd like you to do it."

Stone obliged, and she stepped out of her panties. "Now what?"

"Now you can undress me," Stone said. "That'll give you time to think about what comes next."

She had a little trouble with the three buttons on his cuffs, but she managed. "Now what?"

"That will require a demonstration," he said, leading her to the bed and kissing her again.

"Demonstrate away," she replied.

He did so.

They lay on their backs, panting. "I didn't quite get it,"

Gloria said. "I'll give you a couple of minutes, then I will require another demonstration."

"I admire optimism in a woman," he said.

"Maybe you could use a little help?"

"It couldn't hurt."

She put her face in his lap for a minute or so, then looked up. "My optimism was not misplaced," she said.

Stone demonstrated again, this time with variations, and they managed to reach the end of the demonstration simultaneously.

"Now I get it," Gloria said, throwing a leg over him and nestling against him. "It's a lot like fucking, isn't it?"

"When you're right, you're right," Stone replied.

Stone stirred at his usual time, and he woke her with his tongue.

Ten minutes later, they were both fully awake.

"What's for breakfast?" she asked.

"You name it."

"Well, I've had the first and second courses, could I have a plain omelet, please?"

Stone rang downstairs and placed their order.

"What time is it?"

"Nearly seven."

"I've got a noon deadline for my interview with you."

"Do you have any further questions?" he asked.

"I think you answered them last night, unless I dreamed all those orgasms."

"If you did, then we had the same dream."

"I didn't know that was possible."

"It is, if you work at it."

"I like your work," she said.

Breakfast came, and Stone pressed the button that raised the head of the bed. "So," he said, "my turn for a question."

"Fire away."

"What is your relationship to this guy at Fishkill?"

"We were on our way to a pretty good relationship when he got arrested."

"What was the charge?"

"He was a little vague about that. He said he had sold an apartment for a friend, and it turned out that the friend didn't own it."

"That would attract the attention of the law," Stone observed.

"It did, and as it turned out, it wasn't the first time."

"How did he and his friend get past the closing attorney for the buyer? They wouldn't have had the proper paperwork, would they?"

"As it turned out, the friend had some expertise at closing a sale, until he got disbarred, anyway. He was also pretty good at filling out blank documents and printing others on his computer, and he was also very good at converting cashier's checks to cash in record time."

"How many apartments did they sell?"

"A dozen or so, I believe, mostly between half a million and a million each." She sipped her juice. "This is delicious orange juice."

"It's freshly squoze, like your convict's clients," Stone said.

"I feel freshly squoze myself," she replied.

"Would you like to be squozed again?"

"I would, but not on this occasion. I have to go write up your interview and get it to my editor in time for approval." She gave him a kiss and ran for the shower.

# 9

Stone was curious. Once at his desk he went to NYT.com and typed in "selling real estate you don't own," and got a long story with pictures. The two culprits on trial were Spike Luton, the brains behind the operation, and Danny Blaine, a would-be fashion designer who did the selling. The story was spelled out pretty much as Gloria had told it but included an account of the childhood friendship between the two defendants, including their time done in a juvenile facility for stealing cars and small-time scams.

Danny had actually attended the Fashion Institute of Technology, if only for a couple of semesters, and there had picked up enough credentials to lie about it to prospective employers and unfortunate clients. Although the more willowy of the two, he had exhibited a bent for violence in his teens, carrying a switchblade as a matter of routine. The photograph of him showed a sly, clean-shaven face that reminded Stone of a fox. His original name had been Borgman, before he'd had it legally changed.

He Googled Blaine and came up with a few mentions in gossip columns and photographs at fashion industry parties, one with Gloria Parsons.

He Googled Gloria and found pieces by her for various magazines, the sort of things he would have expected, nothing unusual. The question was, how did she get mixed up with a sleazebag like Blaine? He wasn't sure he wanted to ask her. It had been quite a night, and he found himself already wanting a repeat.

Joan buzzed him. "Dino on one."

Stone pressed the button. "Good morning."

"How was your night?" Dino asked.

"You shared most of it."

"Not your evening, dummy, your night."

"Oh, that. Not exactly disappointing."

Dino laughed. "I thought not. I liked her, she was funny."

"Me, too."

"So you'll see more of her?"

"That would be difficult, but I'm sure we'll enjoy each other's company again."

"I looked up that friend of hers at Fishkill."

"You mean Danny Blaine?"

"You did a little research yourself. What did you think?"

"I thought it was weird that she even knew him."

"You didn't dig deep enough — they were in high school together, and she was briefly implicated in some sort of scam Danny pulled off with his buddy Spike. They were at FIT together, too."

"You're right, I didn't dig deep enough."

Joan buzzed again. "Gloria on two."

"I'll call you back," Stone said to Dino, then pressed two. "Good morning."

"It certainly is," Gloria said. "I wish I were still there."

"Soon enough."

"I've finished my story on you. I'll send you an early copy in a day or two."

"I hope you treated me kindly."

"How could I not, after the way you treated me?"

"I'm glad you enjoyed it."

" 'Enjoy' isn't a strong enough word."

"Same here."

"I've gotta run, my editor is screaming for me."

"Then run."

She hung up, and Stone called Dino back.

"Let me guess," Dino said, "she was

thanking you for the ride last night."

"More or less."

"Did you ask her about Danny?"

"I think I'll wait and let her bring it up. She's pretty talkative."

"Let me know if you need any more research on Danny Blaine."

"I'll do that." They said goodbye and hung up.

Joan buzzed again. "The secretary of state on line one."

Stone pressed the button. "Well, good morning," he said, with warmth.

The response was businesslike. "Will you accept a call from Secretary Barker?"

"Of course," Stone said.

"Good morning."

"Good morning, Madam Secretary, haven't I seen you on a TV show?"

"Not yet, but stick around."

"How's the state of the world today?"

"Have you got a couple of weeks? I'll brief you."

"As bad as that?"

"Nearly as bad. I've had half a dozen texts from people who saw our photo op in the *Debater* yesterday, mostly those who were at our party."

"And what was the response?"

"Uniformly favorable. Maybe being in the

papers wasn't a bad idea — it saves a lot of explaining about who you are."

"When I got home yesterday I had a stack of calls waiting from the media."

"And how did you handle that?"

"Somebody advised me to pick one and tell the rest I'd given them an exclusive."

"Who did you pick?"

"*Just Folks,* a name which I interpreted as being an ironic take on *People.*"

"You could have done worse. What did you tell them?"

"Nothing they couldn't have learned by Googling you."

"All the way back to Orchid Beach?"

"Briefly. Look at it this way — it will be good publicity for your upcoming autobiographical work."

"Oh, we're starting that far ahead, are we?"

"Remember what P. T. Barnum said, '. . . as long as they spell your name right.' "

"I suppose so, and I suppose I'll get used to it. CIA would have frowned upon it, in the old days."

"Those days are gone forever."

"Well, I have to stop a war somewhere. Let's talk now and then, huh?"

"As often as you like. You call me — you're busier than I am."

"You can say that again. Bye." She hung up.

Joan buzzed again. "You're still getting a lot of calls from media types, which I haven't put through. What do you want me to tell them?"

"Tell them to go away, I'm not talking."

"You talked to *Just Folks.*"

"That was so I could tell the others I had given the magazine an exclusive. Try that and see if it works."

"You betcha."

# 10

Stone had a sandwich for lunch at his desk and was still picking his teeth when Joan buzzed. "There's a Mr. Alphonse Teppi to see you on a legal matter. You don't know him."

In the second before he spoke Stone recalled that some interesting turns in his life had arisen from seeing unknown walk-ins, and anyway, he was bored. "Send him in."

Alphonse Teppi was tall and slim, dressed in a beautifully cut Italian suit and an outrageous necktie. "Al Teppi," he said, offering his hand.

Stone shook it. "Have a seat, Mr. Teppi."

Teppi did. "Since we don't know each other, I'd better introduce myself."

"Go right ahead."

"I have a number of clients who call on my services to help select advisors for them."

"What sort of advisors?"

"Agents, publicists, tax accountants, and, sometimes, attorneys."

"Are you an attorney, Mr. Teppi?"

"Sadly, no, though I would have made a good one."

In Stone's experience people had an assortment of strange ideas when it came to judging the qualities of an attorney. "Why do you think that, Mr. Teppi?"

"A reasonable question," Teppi replied. "Because all too often, in dealing with attorneys, it is my own ideas rather than theirs that turn out to be the better way to resolve situations."

"Do you take that view with, say, surgeons?"

*"Negativo,"* Teppi replied, with a small smile.

Stone wondered if that was an Italian word, or if Teppi had just made it up. "Well, let's start with your telling me the problem, and then I'll render an opinion on whether you should consult an attorney or just save the fees and handle it yourself."

"Very well. I have a client who is, for reasons not entirely of his own doing, in an institution upstate."

"Medical? Mental?"

"Penal."

"Ah. And you wish me to get him a new trial?"

"Oh, nothing as long and drawn out as that, I hope. I just want you to get him out."

"Well, if you want fast action, there are, generally speaking, two ways to go — a pardon or a jailbreak. I expect this is where you begin to offer suggestions, is it not?"

"Normally, yes, but I confess I have come up short in that regard. I suppose I was thinking in terms of, ah, influence."

"Influence of whom?"

"Oh, judges, politicians — like that."

"Well, with judges it's considered de rigueur in the legal game to bribe them before the verdict comes in, not later. As for politicians, their role in these things is usually to bribe a judge before the fact, or a governor, afterward."

"I'm not explaining myself very clearly, am I, Mr. Barrington?"

"On the contrary, Mr. Teppi, not only have you been clear but admirably economical and direct in your choice of words. Attorneys appreciate that sort of thing when hearing from prospective clients. It saves so much time."

"Let me rephrase. I had hoped that you might know someone, who knows someone, who knows an official who might be in a position, as a favor, to end my client's confinement or, if not, then to ease the terms under which he is confined."

"Well, as regards ending his confinement, I believe I've already covered the two most commonly employed methods. But if you want your client to have a job in the prison library, a single-occupancy cell, and a bodyguard in the yard, then I think you should think inside the box rather than out."

"Inside the box?"

"The box being the one your client is in."

"Oh. You mean someone who works in the prison?"

"Those are the people inside the box and in charge of the distribution of comforts your client wishes to acquire."

Teppi appeared to be giving this idea considerable thought. "Perhaps, Mr. Barrington, you might describe for me, hypothetically, of course, how this might be achieved."

"Well, hypothetically, of course, one might travel to the municipality in which the box is located and look for a tavern nearby that is frequented by employees of the institution, then spend a few nights drinking there and buying rounds for the other patrons, until a likely candidate emerges from the fog of unfamiliarity, then seek his advice, taking care, of course, to avoid any speech that might be interpreted as suborning a public official, which could lead to one joining one's client inside the box."

"Is that really all you can suggest, Mr. Barrington?"

"Or," Stone said, "your client could adapt himself to his environment, allow the staff to find him earnest and cooperative, and let good behavior work its magic on the length of his sentence. Otherwise, I would advise him to avoid fights and bending over in the shower, unless he wishes to invite the attentions that that sort of behavior elicits."

Stone placed his palms on his desk and rose. "Now, Mr. Teppi, unless you wish me to draw your will or perform some other *conventional* legal service, I believe I have done all I can do for you."

Teppi rose slowly and thoughtfully and shook Stone's hand again. "Thank you for the courtesy of your time, Mr. Barrington." He turned to go.

"Oh, Mr. Teppi, might the name of your client be Danny Blaine?"

Teppi blinked. "Why, yes," he said.

"I rather thought it might be," Stone replied, then he sat down and pretended to work until Alphonse Teppi had made his exit.

When Stone had stopped chuckling to himself, he phoned Dino.

"Bacchetti."

"Dino, have you ever heard of someone called Alphonse Teppi?"

The clicking of computer keys ensued. "All I can tell you about him is that he has never been arrested," Dino said. "Why do you ask?"

"Because a person calling himself that just walked into my office and pretty much asked me, straight out, to bribe Danny Blaine out of Fishkill."

"How much did you charge him?" Dino asked.

"Let me put it this way — my boot may still be lodged in his ass."

"You're such a disappointment to me, Stone. You and I could have dined out for a year on the proceeds of that conversation."

# 11

Stone and Gloria Parsons were dining out at Rôtisserie Georgette, uptown from him, and were awaiting delivery of a plump roast hen. They were on their second drink.

"Now that we're all settled in," he said, "tell me how your Mr. Teppi came to believe that I would bribe people to get your pal Danny out of Fishkill."

"Mr. Teppi has a mind of his own," she replied smoothly.

"Then tell me how he came to choose me to make his proposal."

"I may have mentioned your name in passing."

"Kindly refrain from mentioning my name to such people," he said, "in passing or in any regard."

"I have just mentioned it to some three million people," she said, "and that is only in the contiguous forty-eight states."

"What's the matter, are there no pseudo-sophisticates in Alaska, Hawaii, Puerto Rico, and Samoa?"

"They're not worth the postage," she replied. She withdrew a magazine from her purse and handed it across the table. "Come to think of it, neither are you, so I'm delivering it personally."

Stone was greeted with the photograph of Holly and himself taken in Georgetown. "Jesus Christ," he said.

"What's the matter, don't you enjoy being a cover girl?"

"I had imagined this would rate a column or less on the page with the truss and erectile dysfunction ads," he said, flipping the magazine open and finding that the interview with him covered three and a half pages, with photos from his college yearbook, his NYPD ID, one next to an old airplane, and one from his extreme youth, of him playing touch football in Central Park in which all the other players were girls. "Where the hell did you come up with all this?"

"Well, I did take a rather nice one of you naked on your back in bed, but my editor said you weren't well endowed enough for our centerfold."

"Please thank her for her discretion."

"I'll pass it along."

"When I read this, am I going to want to sue you?"

"I hope that what you will want to do to me *rhymes* with 'sue,' " she said, tickling his crotch with a stockinged toe.

He laughed in spite of himself. "I want you to stop that fairly soon."

Their chicken was presented, and they began dismembering it.

"To get back to Mr. Blaine, why the hell are you so hot to get him out? From what I've read about him, he richly deserves his sentence."

"He is my friend, and I am a loyal person."

"If you aren't careful you're going to end up in a cell of your own for your efforts on his behalf. I mean, Mr. Teppi could have contacted an attorney who has the police commissioner for a friend."

"Those are the chances one must take to help a friend."

"What about his partner in crime, Spike Whatshisname? Is he an old high school chum, as well?"

"Danny is my friend. Spike is Danny's. It stops there."

"Tell me, what happened to the millions these two filched from eager home buyers?"

She stopped chewing. "Do you suspect me of dark motives?"

"I was trained as a cop, I reflexively suspect people of darker motives than friendship."

"I suspect they spent it on booze and loose women," she said. "Neither of them has ever struck me as an investor."

"A dozen or more apartments that sold for between half a million and a million — that's a ton of money when you add it up. Did they have expensive lawyers?"

"I doubt it. They suggested that I might contribute to their defense fund, but I declined. Whoever they hired advised them to plead out, and it doesn't take a Stone Barrington to handle that."

"Do they really think you can get them out?"

"There's no 'them,' for me, just Danny. Spike can go rot, for all I care. Danny has a child-like faith in me, and I dislike disappointing him."

"What other jams have you gotten him out of over the years of your cherished friendship?"

"Nothing that a little flirting with a school principal couldn't fix."

"I'm sure you could bat your eyelashes and his eyes would glaze over."

"You're a good judge of character," she replied.

The waiter spirited away the remains of the chicken and brought a complimentary dessert from Georgette.

"By the way," she said as he paid the bill, "I argued with my editor about your endowment."

"Oh?"

"I explained to her that skill trumps size."

"That's very sweet of you. I hope that didn't make it into your piece."

"It's not information I would want to share with our readers," she said. "You might never have time to see me again."

"Well, we can't have that, can we? What are you doing right now?"

"I am at your disposal," she replied.

Stone ran outside and threw himself in front of a cab.

# 12

Stone was at his desk the following morning, feeling a little sore from his exertions the previous night, when Joan buzzed him.

"Madam Secretary on one for you."

Stone pressed the button. "Yes?"

"Will you speak to Secretary Barker?" the chilly woman asked.

"At all times," he replied, "you don't need to ask."

"I need to ask at all times, Mr. Barrington," she replied, and there was a click.

"Good morning."

"And good morning to you, Madam Secretary."

"I'm getting used to being called that," she said.

"All right," he said, "but never in bed."

"Careful."

He hadn't thought about that. "Still saving the world?"

"Every day, from seven to seven more or

less. I had a call from Kate's secretary this morning. She and the family are available for a holiday cruise." She suggested dates.

"Confirmed," Stone said.

"They would like to fly into Key West Naval Air Station, then take a helicopter from there directly to the yacht, which should be docked at the Coast Guard facility in Key West.

"She also said that they prefer not to use a naval or Coast Guard vessel as an escort, since they might attract the attention of the media. Instead, they have asked the secretary of the Navy to look through his inventory and see if the Navy possesses a motor yacht of a suitable size that could be used."

"A sensible suggestion. I hadn't thought about a Coast Guard cutter attracting attention."

"Just between us, since the close election, death threats directed at the First Family have been received, and they are being particularly careful about personal travel."

"I'm sorry to hear that, and I understand their concerns. Will you be flying in with them, or shall I transport you myself?"

"If it is convenient, could you pick up Peter, Celeste, and me at Manassas and fly us to Key West to meet the yacht on the day?"

"I'd be delighted to, Manassas is on the way."

"Oh, and Kate suggests that if there's room, you invite Dino and Vivian Bacchetti to join us."

"There is room, and I will invite them. They can fly down with us."

"And she will be traveling at all times with two Secret Service agents as body people, and they will need to stay aboard. How many cabins are there?"

"Seven, so we will have three spares available, should she need to bring a secretary or maybe a food taster."

"I'll let her know. Oh, there'll also be a naval officer aboard who is in charge of the football."

"There's a large, open upper deck, but it's not really suitable for sports."

"I refer to the suitcase that travels everywhere with the President, containing the codes and communications for nuclear war."

"Oh. Well, it looks as though we will have a full complement of passengers, then. I'll let the chef know."

"The Secret Service and any staff can dine with the crew," Holly said. "The Secret Service will need to inspect the yacht, of course, and I'm told a small amount of communications equipment will need to be brought aboard. They'll need a full day."

"Then they can have their day."

"And I'll need the cell phone number of the captain, so that various people can communicate with him in the planning stages."

Stone gave her the captain's name and number.

"I think that's all for the present," she said. "As you can see, all this could be a logistical nightmare if it's not very well planned well in advance."

"I get the picture."

"Are you surviving without me?"

"Barely. Oh, I saw the piece in *Just Folks*. I don't think there's anything that will alarm you."

"Good, I get enough alarms in this job."

They said goodbye and hung up.

Stone called Dino.

"Bacchetti."

"I am required by the President of the United States, on pain of death, to command the presence of the commissioner and Mrs. Bacchetti aboard the yacht *Breeze,* for a holiday cruise with the Presidents Lee and family, departing from Key West, Florida."

There was a brief silence. "Okay," Dino said. "Anything else?"

"We will depart Teterboro for Key West

on my airplane that morning."

"Got it."

"That is all."

"Have you read the thing in *Just Folks*?"

"Sort of."

"Maybe you'd better read it more carefully. See ya." Dino hung up.

Stone reached for the magazine; the item Dino had clearly referred to was near the end.

Stone Barrington has been either a bachelor or a widower for all but a year of his life, a fact well known to a great many women. A dozen or so that this publication spoke to were very complimentary of his style, equipment, and skill. "That combination is very hard to come by," one of them said, sighing. "You should excuse the expression."

Stone sat back in his chair and emitted a sound that combined a groan and a whimper.

"Ah," said Joan, who had been standing in the doorway. "You've read the magazine."

Stone leaned forward and pressed his hot forehead against the cool desktop.

"I'll leave you alone with yourself," Joan

said, and closed the door behind her.

Stone refused all calls for the rest of the day. As Joan was leaving work she stopped by his desk and left a stack of phone slips. "Most of them are from women," she said, "but one of them is from Bill Eggers." Eggers was the managing partner of Woodman & Weld.

"I'll never be able to leave the house again," Stone said, but Joan had already gone.

# 13

Grimly, Stone called Eggers's private line.

He answered himself. "Bill Eggers."

"It's Stone, returning yours."

Eggers emitted a low chuckle. "Stone, all of us at Woodman & Weld, partners and clients alike, would like to congratulate you on exceeding our opinion of you. And in a national magazine!" He roared with laughter, then hung up.

No sooner had Stone set down the phone than the office doorbell began ringing repeatedly. Wearily, he got into his jacket and walked down the hallway past Joan's office to the outside door and unlocked it. A woman he didn't know but who looked vaguely familiar was standing there.

"Come with me, please," she demanded, then turned and started down the sidewalk. She stopped and looked back. "Come with me this instant!"

Stone tried to catch up with her. "I don't

understand," he said.

She stopped two houses down the street, where the front door stood open. "In here!" she said, pointing.

"Madam, I . . ."

"In here!" she shouted.

Stone peered inside, wondering what awaited him. He stepped into an entrance hall and a man wearing a cardigan sweater, reading glasses, and carrying a newspaper appeared from an adjoining room.

"This is my husband," the woman said. "I want you to tell him about the relationship between you and me!"

He looked at her, then back at him. "What relationship? We have no relationship," he said. "I don't know either of you."

"There!" she shouted at her husband. "Is that good enough for you?"

"Yes," the man replied weakly.

She turned toward Stone. "Thank you, you may leave now."

Stone was happy to leave as quickly as possible. He didn't look behind him until his office door was closed and locked.

He went upstairs to his study and poured himself a stiff drink, not bothering with the ice, and sank into a chair before the fireplace. The phone rang, and he glanced at the caller ID: Dino.

He picked it up. "Yeah?"

"Are you drunk yet?" Dino asked.

"No, but I'm making a start."

"I'm in the car. I'll be there in three minutes."

"In the study," Stone said. Three minutes later the doorbell rang, and he buzzed it open.

Dino came into the study, poured himself a stiff scotch, and sat down. "You okay?" he asked, tapping Stone's glass with his own.

"No," Stone replied, "I feel like I've been struck with an ax handle."

"Like in the bar fight in *Shane*?"

"Exactly like that. Do you know, a woman who lives a couple of doors down the street just rang the downstairs doorbell and insisted I come to her house, address her husband, and tell him we weren't having an affair? I'd never clapped eyes on either of them."

Dino dissolved in laughter. "What did you say to him?" he asked, when he had recovered enough.

"What do you think I said to him? I denied everything."

Dino laughed again.

"Joan gave me a stack of messages, all from women except one from Bill Eggers."

"What was Bill's reaction?"

"Pretty much the same as yours." Stone downed half his drink.

Dino tossed off his drink and stood up, grasping Stone by the arm and hauling him to his feet. "Come with me," he said.

Stone put down his drink, followed him to the door and outside, where his SUV awaited. "Where are we going?"

"Out to dinner," Dino replied, thrusting him into the rear seat. "To Clarke's." He got in.

"I can't go out in public," Stone said.

"You have to, pal, there's only one way to handle this — brazen it through."

"Oh, Jesus."

They were deposited on the sidewalk outside P. J. Clarke's. "Neutral face," Dino said, placing a hand in the small of his back and propelling him forward. "Don't make eye contact."

They stepped inside, and as the door closed behind them half the room went silent and stared, while the other half chatted on as before. Dino led the way toward the dining room, holding up two fingers for the maître d'. They were at a table in seconds.

Dino ordered the drinks. "Now, that wasn't so bad, was it?"

"It was horrible," Stone said.

"Smile," Dino said.

"At what?"

"Just smile."

Stone managed a toothy grimace.

"That's better." A waitress approached. "Two New York strips, medium, fries, a bottle of the Châteauneuf-du-Pape," he said to the young woman.

"You're Stone Barrington, aren't you?" she asked slyly.

"You bet your sweet ass he is," Dino said. "Food!"

She hurried away.

After Stone had eaten his steak and drunk two glasses of wine, he felt better.

"You're coming around, I can tell," Dino said.

"I feel nearly normal," Stone said.

The waitress came back with two slices of apple pie. "On me," she said, with a broad smile and a wink.

"Has Holly seen the magazine?" Dino asked.

"God, I hope not."

"Well, you can hope."

"I told her it was inoffensive."

"It was inoffensive, you just aren't used to seeing yourself described in print. Do you know what names I've been called since I got this job and the media suddenly found out who I was?"

"That's different."

"No, it's not. At least *Just Folks* was complimentary."

"If I try to eat that pie I'm going to throw up," Stone said.

"Take one bite — you don't want to insult the woman. Then we'll get out of here."

Stone choked down a bite, and Dino got them out of there and back into his car. Shortly they were at Stone's front door.

"Don't drink any more tonight," Dino said, "or you'll have a terrible hangover in the morning, and that will make things even worse."

"Thanks for the advice," Stone said. He got the front door open, went upstairs, stripped, and fell into bed.

The phone rang, but he didn't answer it.

# 14

Stone sat down at his desk and began to make work motions. Joan came in and inspected him closely. "You're not as hung over as I thought you'd be."

"Dino got me through the evening. He insisted we go out in public."

"Exactly the right thing to do."

"Joan, do you know who the people are, two doors down the street, to the left?"

"No clue."

"I want you to order a dozen red roses and have them left on the doorstep, with a card reading 'Darling, I can't wait to see you.' "

"Stone, do you know these people?"

"No, but they seem to know me all of a sudden. Make sure the flowers can't be traced to me."

"I'll buy them at the Korean market and deliver them myself."

"Just leave them on the doorstep."

"As you wish."

"And if anybody asks, you know nothing."

"I always know nothing," she replied, then left the room. Stone heard the outside door close a minute later. He went through yesterday's messages and didn't find a single one that wasn't from a woman he didn't know.

The phone rang, and since Joan was out rose shopping, he answered. "Stone Barrington."

"It's Gloria."

"Go away," he said, and hung up. A couple of minutes later it rang again. "Stone Barrington."

"It was a joke," she said. "Tell you what, I'll make it up to you this evening."

"It was a bad joke," he said. "And it's made my life miserable. I meant it when I said go away, and if you ever print my name in your rag again, I'll make *your* life miserable." He hung up emphatically.

Joan came back. "The roses are delivered," she said.

"Good. Now lock the front door, and don't open it to anyone bearing roses, male or female. And if Gloria Parsons ever calls again, don't say a word, just hang up, and if she calls back, keep hanging up."

"Gotcha," Joan said, sounding pleased.

The phone rang, and Joan picked up. "The Barrington Group." She covered the receiver. "Madam Secretary on one."

Stone picked up. "Yes, I'll speak to her."

"You are speaking to her," Holly said.

"Oh. I'd grown accustomed to something more formal."

"I had a word with her."

"Thank you."

"I finally got around to reading the piece in *Just Folks.*"

"I'm sorry about that. I hadn't read it thoroughly when I told you it was inoffensive."

"It was inoffensive — to me. How about you?"

"I'd rather not talk about it."

"I don't blame you a bit, and I won't bring it up again. Official change of subject — have you spoken to your yacht captain about our cruise?"

"Not yet."

"Now would be a good time. He'll be getting a lot of calls, and he needs to be warned that all this is top secret, and he could end up in Leavenworth if he or any of his crew blabs to anybody at all, at sea or ashore."

"I'll get that done right away."

"Are you all right, Stone? You sound a little depressed."

"I was a little depressed. I'm better now."

"Good. Take care."

Stone looked up the number of the yacht's captain and called.

"Good morning, this is Captain Joe."

"Good morning, Captain, this is Stone Barrington. How are you?"

"Very well, Mr. Barrington. What can I do for you?"

"Got a pencil?"

"Yes."

"Please have the yacht in Key West on the first day, docked at the Coast Guard facility and ready for a serious going-over."

"Yes, sir."

"I hope that won't interfere with your holiday schedule or that of your crew."

"No, sir, it won't. How long a cruise?"

"A week, itinerary to be determined, but we will want to visit mostly isolated places around the Keys."

"How about Fort Jefferson?"

"That's west of Key West?"

"Yes. It's a pre–Civil War fort, nicely restored. Dr. Samuel Mudd, who set John Wilkes Booth's leg after the Lincoln assassination, was imprisoned there and became a hero for putting down a yellow fever epidemic."

"I recall that from my school days."

"It's very isolated, only a few daily visitors by yacht and a daily seaplane. Gorgeous beach on a neighboring island, nobody on it."

"Ideal."

"I can find other interesting anchorages, as well."

"Good. Are any of your crew not American citizens?"

"Our cook is Italian, but she has a green card."

"Good. You're going to get a call — perhaps many calls — from the United States Secret Service, and they're going to want the name, date of birth, and Social Security number of each of your crew."

"Roger."

"Are you beginning to get the idea, Cap?"

"I believe so, sir."

"Then you'll understand, and impress upon your crew, that they are not to share any information about our cruise with any living person of any persuasion."

"I understand completely. They can be very closemouthed. How many persons will be aboard?"

"Four couples, no children or dogs, two Secret Service agents, and one naval officer carrying communications equipment. We will be escorted by another motor yacht, description to be determined, carrying other government personnel and equipment."

"Got it."

"Our guests of honor will land at the Key West Naval Air Station and be transported to the Coast Guard station by helicopter and will be berthed in the owner's cabin. I and my companion will take the aft cabin. The other two couples will be in the next two best cabins. Our party will land at Key West International and take cabs to the yacht. With everyone aboard, perhaps we should anchor off somewhere for dinner that evening and depart for Fort Jefferson the following morning."

"I'll pick a quiet place."

"The Secret Service and naval personnel will take their meals with the crew. During their inspection, in addition to their thorough look at the yacht, they will install some communications equipment, which will go with them when they leave. Please give them every assistance."

"I will certainly do so. Will we have to deal with any press?"

"Not if everyone keeps his mouth shut. I will consider it a moral failure if any media show up. No need to mention any of this to your crew, until you are approaching Key West."

"I understand perfectly."

"Call me on my cell if you have any questions or concerns."

"Yes, sir."

Both men hung up. The captain seemed to get it, Stone reflected.

# 15

By the following morning Stone's depression had cleared away like an afternoon thunderstorm.

Dino called. "Better?"

"Better," Stone said. "Normal, in fact."

"Good, then Viv and I can invite you to Thanksgiving dinner at our place without worrying about your spoiling everyone's good time."

"Thank you, I'd love to."

"Why don't you invite Holly?"

"I will do so."

"We got an invitation to Peter Rule's wedding reception," Dino said. "It's in New York."

Stone fumbled through the mail stacked on his desk. "Got it," he said. It was being held the Sunday evening after Thanksgiving at the Metropolitan Club, in New York. "I assume you'll be there."

"If we've recovered from Thanksgiving

dinner," Dino said. "Viv is cooking."

"Hire a caterer."

"She won't have it — something about the way her mother did it."

"Hire a crew of reinforcements, then."

"Good idea. Gotta run." He hung up.

Stone checked the reception invitation again, then asked Joan to call Madam Secretary.

"On the line," Joan said.

"Good morning, Madam Secretary."

"Talk fast, the British ambassador is on hold."

"Come to New York for Thanksgiving dinner at Dino and Viv's and the wedding reception."

"See you on the Wednesday afternoon," she said.

"I'll send a gift from both of us."

"Great, bye." She moved on to the British ambassador.

Stone went online to the Tiffany website and viewed the sterling silver patterns, then ordered twelve place settings of the very plain Faneuil pattern and a suitable chest in cherry and had them sent with a card from Holly and him. He liked to get that sort of thing out of the way before he forgot about it.

Joan buzzed him. "A Mr. Edward Cumming to see you."

Another walk-in. "Oh, what the hell, send him in."

Mr. Edward Cumming had brought a friend. The two of them were in their mid-thirties and would have answered to the same police description: medium height, medium weight, medium everything. Stone offered them chairs. "What can I do for you, gentlemen?"

Both men produced badges. "We are senior investigators with the Criminal Investigation Division of the New York State Police," one of them said. "My name is Cumming, my partner is Malloy."

"How do you do?" Stone said.

"Not as well as you do," Cumming said, looking around the office.

"Thank you, I think," Stone replied.

"Our office has had a report that you have offered advice to a client on how to illegally secure a pardon or special treatment for an inmate of the New York State Prison System, one Daniel Blaine."

"That is preposterous," Stone replied.

"Are you acquainted with one Alphonse Teppi?"

" 'Acquainted' is too strong a word," Stone replied. "The gentleman you refer to walked into my office three days ago and hinted that he wanted such advice. After a brief conversation, during which I offered no illegal advice apart from cautioning him not to break the law, Mr. Teppi left my office at my invitation. I did not accept him as a client, and I have not seen or heard from him before or since."

"What would you say if I told you I had a recording of your entire conversation?" Cumming asked.

"I would say that such a recording, if undoctored, would confirm the facts I have just related to you."

"Would you say that the recording might contain advice, perhaps offered with sarcasm, in such matters?"

"I would say that, as a matter of personal preference, I might respond to ridiculous requests with sarcasm, perhaps heavy sarcasm, and that I probably did so on that occasion before I requested Mr. Teppi's departure from my office."

"Exactly how did you frame your request, Mr. Barrington?"

"I believe I stood up and said, 'Good day,' or words to that effect."

Cumming placed a small recording device on Stone's desk and switched it on. It played a recording of his conversation with Teppi. When it finished, Cumming switched it off. "Is that an undoctored version of your conversation with Mr. Teppi?"

"It appears to be," Stone replied.

"In light of what you have just heard, would you like to alter your answers to my questions in any way?"

"No," Stone replied. "I believe the recording supports my statements to you."

Cumming exchanged a glance with his colleague, who gave him a small nod. "We accept your account and intent with regard to the recording."

"May I have a recording of that statement?" Stone asked, and to their credit, both men laughed.

"Mr. Barrington," Cumming said, "do you know why Teppi sought you out or who referred him to you?"

Stone thought about that for a moment. "Gentlemen, the recording contains no mention of that."

"I'll grant you that, Mr. Barrington, but my question remains the same — do you know who referred Mr. Teppi to you?"

"I have no exact knowledge of that, and I will refrain from guessing," Stone replied, "but surely Mr. Teppi knows who referred him to me. Why don't you ask him?"

"We have already done so, and his only answer was that the referral came from an acquaintance at a prominent magazine. He would not divulge the name."

"I have no basis on which to argue with Mr. Teppi's answer to your question," Stone said.

"Would you care to hazard a guess as to what person at which magazine?"

"I would not."

"Would it, perhaps, be a Ms. Parsons at *Just Folks* magazine?"

"Given the state of my knowledge, I could neither confirm nor deny that."

"Are you acquainted with Ms. Parsons?"

"I was, briefly. I no longer am."

"Do you mean that you know her, but you do not wish to know her?"

"I think that's a fair characterization of my meaning."

"Then I think we need not take up any more of your time, Mr. Barrington." Both men got up and left.

Stone buzzed Joan.

"Yes, boss?"

"If that character Alphonse Teppi shows up again or calls, please show him the same courtesy I asked you to show Gloria Parsons."

# 16

Holly Barker arrived at mid-afternoon on the Wednesday before Thanksgiving, having borne before her two large pieces of luggage, a matching makeup bag, and an unmatching, bulging briefcase bearing the seal of the secretary of state. She gave Stone a kiss, then spent half an hour transferring the contents of her luggage to her dressing room, then occupied Stone's study for two hours of pawing at the briefcase and making and receiving calls on her cell phone.

Stone came up at six and stood in the doorway, observing her last five minutes at work. Finally, she switched off her phone, jumped from her chair, and threw herself at him, along with a very large kiss. "There," she said, "may I have a drink now?"

"You may," Stone replied, handing her a large Knob Creek on the rocks and fixing himself one. They flopped down onto the sofa before the fireplace, clinked glasses, drank, then looked at each other fondly. "You made it," Stone said.

"I did."

"I expected a last-minute call, canceling, with very good reasons."

"My presence was never in doubt," she said.

"Did you travel up on a bus?"

"I traveled on a helicopter the Air Force is kind enough to make available from time to time."

"And where is your security entourage?"

"At home with their families, I hope. I dismissed them for the weekend, with some difficulty. I had to sign a document relieving them of any responsibility for anything you might do to me."

Stone laughed. "How specific did you get?"

"It was a general sort of description that covered just about everything."

"Well, just about everything is what I'm planning to do to you."

"I had hoped for that, starting right after dinner, because I had my hair done earlier today and would not wish to sacrifice it to the god of sex."

"Duly noted."

"Where are we dining?"

"I thought I would force a large hunk of

beef on you at Patroon."

"Yummy."

"Tomorrow is Thanksgiving dinner at the hands of Vivian Bacchetti — something about what her mother would do in the same circumstances, I believe. Then we have the rest of the weekend to lie around in bed, sending out for pizza and other delicacies, as necessary. We won't be due anywhere until Sunday evening at the Metropolitan Club."

"That is as perfect a Thanksgiving holiday as a girl could ask for."

"I had hoped you would think so."

"Just so I know, what gift did we bestow upon the newlyweds?"

"Twelve place settings of Tiffany silver."

"Which pattern?"

"Faneuil."

"Such elegant simplicity!"

"And in years to come we can give them matching serving pieces, et cetera."

"How clever of you, not to mention lazy."

"We didn't get an invitation to the wedding. When is or was it?"

"Tomorrow, in the family quarters of the White House, attended only by family. Kate thought a blowout in the East Room would be overdoing it, since Peter is only a son. The father of the bride is a member of the

Metropolitan, hence its choice. After all, he is — and his son-in-law hopes to be — a senator from New York, so best to have the reception here."

"How many guests?" Stone asked.

"As many as the ballroom will hold, I imagine."

"And that will be a great many, since it eats up about a hundred feet of Fifth Avenue."

"There will be a big band, so you will have to dance with me."

"And I shall."

"No boogying, don't worry."

"Do you think me incapable of boogying?"

"I think you unwilling to."

"You have a point."

"Unless you are very, very drunk and that, in itself, would obviate boogying."

"A fine point, well made."

She set down her drink. "May I excuse myself to dress for dinner? It takes longer than it did before you bought me a new wardrobe."

"You are excused."

Fred drove them to the restaurant so that Holly would not have to hoof it in very high heels, and deposited them on the sidewalk.

They left their coats in the car.

Then they walked into the restaurant and experienced something new — for Stone, at least. Someone began to clap, others joined in, and soon they were receiving a standing ovation.

Holly leaned in to Stone. "Is this for Madam Secretary or for your newly revealed sexual prowess?"

That had not occurred to Stone.

"You're blushing," she said as the applause died and they were led by Ken Aretsky, the owner, to a favored booth, visible from anywhere in the restaurant. Drinks materialized.

"I love this place," Holly said.

"And it loves you, as it has just demonstrated."

"How many women have you brought here, Stone?"

"You are the two hundred and eleventh, if memory serves."

Stone ordered Caesar salads and Chateaubriand for two. Ken Aretsky appeared with a bottle of wine and presented it, a Château Mouton Rothschild 1978, with its label by Jean-Paul Riopelle. "With our compliments."

Stone accepted with a nod, and Aretsky produced a lighted candle and decanted the wine for them.

Stone tasted a little. "Magnificent," he said.

Dinner arrived.

"Remember," Holly said, "we have to eat Thanksgiving dinner in only seventeen hours, or so."

"We'll skip breakfast," Stone said, digging in.

They arrived home pleasantly drunk, disrobed, and engaged, then engaged again.

"Your reputation precedes you," Holly said.

# 17

Stone and Holly arrived at Dino and Viv's Park Avenue apartment on schedule. Many hugs and kisses ensued.

"The wine you sent arrived," Viv said to Stone, "but if we serve it, our guests will think Dino is on the take."

"A simple, unpretentious California Cabernet," Stone said.

"Caymus Special Selection? Simple? Unpretentious?"

Stone looked around at the collection of retired police officers and politicians. "Most of your guests will never have heard of or really appreciate it," Stone said. "Still, it's nice to be good to them. When they taste it they'll approve."

"They'd better," Viv replied.

"I was led to believe we would find you only in the kitchen," Stone said.

"Dino, the angel, hired a support team. All I have to do is instruct them or, maybe, slap them around a little. If my mother were here, she'd believe she cooked it all."

"I can't wait."

"Holly," Viv said, "you look fabulous!"

"When I was appointed, the President insisted I dress like a grown-up," Holly replied.

"Some grown-up!"

Dino extracted himself from a nest of blue suits and joined them. "Stone, the wine is sensational! Did you make it yourself?"

"My feet are still red from the crushing of the grapes."

"I heard you had a visit from our colleagues at the state police."

"I did."

"It was true, as I told you, that Teppi had never been arrested, but, as it turns out, he's been questioned more than a dozen times. The slippery type."

"All too clear."

"I ran Gloria Parsons's name, too, but all we could convict her of is sleazy journalism."

"That's pretty clear, too."

"I heard you got a standing ovation at Patroon last night."

"That was for Holly."

"That's not how I heard it."

"I hope to God you're wrong."

"I think it was for Stone, too," Holly said.

The Bacchettis were pulled away in different directions and Stone and Holly found themselves afloat in a collection of Hermès neckties and large wristwatches. The wives all seemed to be clad in red.

They found seats at a card table, which saved them from having to eat from their laps, and the food was as good as Viv's mother would have expected. It was hard not to eat too much, and when they left at half past three, Viv pressed a box of leftovers on them. "So you won't have to dine out tonight."

As they left the building they encountered a knot of media types and a couple of TV cameras confined to the gutter by half a dozen NYPD uniforms. Strobe lights flashed, and Stone caught a glimpse of Alphonse Teppi in the middle of the throng, for no apparent reason.

"Who's the lizard?" Holly asked.

"He is what he appears to be," Stone said. "He came to see me and suggested that I somehow get some acquaintances of his released from prison, and the sonofabitch recorded the conversation, which was played back to me by a couple of New York State cops. Fortunately, I was sufficiently abusive of him as to appear innocent in their eyes."

"Is that the Teppi Dino mentioned?"

"Try and forget his name."

Fred had the car door open, and they were inside before too many photos could be taken.

"I hope you're getting used to the attention of the media," Stone said.

"It seems to happen only when I'm with you."

They took a drive down Fifth Avenue on the way home; the trees in Central Park were mostly bare but showed a lingering bit of color here and there.

"I miss the leaves," Holly said.

"They'll be back in the spring — happens every year."

Viv had been right, they dined in the late evening on leftovers and a good bottle of wine. Later, in bed, they found a movie on TV.

"I'm glad you're not a football nut," Holly said.

"Only when I care who wins. NYU didn't have a football team."

"Did you notice that there was a gang of men in Dino's study watching a game?"

"It's the Thanksgiving affliction," Stone replied.

# 18

On Friday, Holly flung herself into the loot-
ing of Madison Avenue and, on her way
home, Bloomingdale's. She arrived home
empty-handed.

"All that and no shopping bags?" Stone
asked.

"I sent it all. It was mostly clothes for
work, more businesslike things than I'm accustomed to."

"Congrats on sending everything — that's
what FedEx is for, isn't it?"

They ordered in Chinese food from up the
street and ate too much.

"I'm not going to be able to get into my
ball gown," Holly said.

"You're wearing a ball gown?"

"It's that kind of event, Stone. All you
have to worry about is pressing your tuxedo."

"Already pressed."

On Sunday evening, Fred dropped them at One East Sixtieth Street. There was a delay because of the line of limos. It had begun to snow lightly, so they checked their coats.

The crowd was aglitter with bright colors and serious jewelry. "I reckon this crowd is divided among family friends, the one-tenth of one percent, and the political types from upstate, who will be important to Peter's election to the Senate."

"How do you figure out which ones are the upstate politicians?"

"They're wearing clip-on bow ties and wingtips with their tuxes."

She looked around. "That is an astute observation."

Then someone was tugging at Stone's elbow. He turned to find Gloria Parsons with her notebook and gold pen in hand, showing too much cleavage. "Good evening!" she said brightly.

Stone smiled, since camera flashes were going off. "Get out of my sight," he said softly.

"Aren't you going to introduce me to the secretary of state?"

"I am not, and if you don't go away, I'll have the Secret Service throw you out into the street."

She took a step back, and her smile became a snarl. "You don't know who you're messing with," she hissed.

"I know exactly who and what you are." Stone looked around for a man with a little badge in his lapel and a microphone in his ear. There was one six feet away. "Agent?" he said in a normal voice.

The man stepped over. "Yes, sir?"

"This . . . *person* is annoying the secretary of state. Would you be kind enough to remove her?"

"Yes, Mr. Barrington," the man said. He stepped deftly between Stone and Parsons, took her by the wrist, and tucked her arm over his, as if he were escorting her to dinner. "Right this way, madam," he said, and began towing her toward the door.

"But I'm press," Parsons protested, holding up her invitation.

The agent reached over and plucked it from her hand. "Not anymore," he said, quickening his pace.

Stone and Holly watched as she stopped at the door, stamped her foot, and handed him a ticket. He looked at it, handed it to another agent, and waited while he got her coat. He helped her on with it, then through the door and outside into the snow.

"Nicely done," Holly said. "I suspect that was the woman from *Just Folks.*"

"You suspect correctly," he said. "She won't get back in here tonight. How did that agent know my name?"

"He knows my name," Holly replied. "You're on the list as my escort."

"Ah." He led her toward the grand ballroom. "I see they're confining the media to the foyer," he said. "We will have peace inside."

They got their table number from the reception table and worked their way through a receiving line manned by the happy parents — one of them a United States senator — the President of the United States and her husband, the former President of the United States, and in the middle, the happy couple, Mr. and Mrs. Peter Rule, she, née Celeste Saltonstall. Everyone was happy to see everyone else.

Immediately, they began to run into people they knew: Stone knew the New Yorkers, Holly, the Washingtonians, and they busied themselves with introductions. They saw senators from a dozen states and God-knew-how-many congressmen, all with their wives.

They passed into the ballroom, which was

everything in the way of Italian Renaissance design that the eminent turn-of-the-twentieth-century architect Stanford White could throw at it. The room was ornate and much of it was gilded. Many dining tables had been set around a large dance floor, and at one end what appeared to be the entire New York Pops orchestra was leaning into a Strauss waltz.

"This is as grand as Americans know how to make it," Stone said. "To do better, we'd need a king, a queen, and an aristocracy to show us how."

"We do have an aristocracy," Holly said, "based mostly on money, and we're standing in the middle of some of it."

Stone took her hand, snaked an arm around her waist, launched her into a Viennese waltz, buoyed along by the big string section. "I thought we'd get this out of the way early, before the floor is jammed with the competition."

"I should have known you'd know how to waltz." Holly laughed, throwing her head back and enjoying the moment. The waltz ended, mercifully, just before Stone would have broken a sweat, and they found their way to their table. Along the Fifth Avenue side of the room, the family party had split up and each member hosted a table. Stone and Holly drew Peter Rule, who was seated between them.

Earlier in the week, Stone had hosted Peter at Woodman & Weld, during his visit to get to know the legal team of The Barrington Group and sign on as a client.

"Stone, I very much enjoyed my visit to your firm," Peter said, "and I feel very well taken care of."

"We enjoyed having you," Stone replied, "and we look forward to a long and successful relationship."

Holly told him how beautiful Celeste looked, and they chatted about the origins of her dress for a few minutes.

"How did the wedding go?" Stone asked.

"Since we had to deal with fewer than a dozen guests, it went very quickly, and we had a nice lunch."

"Have you been given Secret Service protection yet?" Stone asked.

"I've managed to avoid it up until now," Peter replied, "because I lived in London for four years. When I came back and went to work for Senator Saltonstall, I still avoided it because I was unknown to the general public, but now, after this and all the resulting press coverage, I will no longer be able to avoid it. Celeste regards their presence as a convenience, someone to hold her shopping bags while doing Madison Avenue, so she doesn't mind, and I suppose I don't mind being driven to work, so I can open my briefcase and get some things done on the way, but I'm sure that, eventually, they're going to become a royal pain in the ass."

"The only way to deal with it is to get used to it," Stone said. "They'll likely be with you for the rest of your life."

Peter looked at Stone as if his secret had been learned. "From your lips to God's ear," he replied.

# 19

Peter leaned toward Stone. "Do you know a woman called Gloria Parsons, from some magazine?"

"Unfortunately," Stone replied. "Half an hour ago I took the liberty of asking a Secret Service agent to throw her out into the street."

"Celeste and I are so grateful to you for that," Peter said. "After seeing what she did to you and Holly, we had her name taken off the press list, but she got in somehow."

"I don't think she'll get back in," Stone replied.

"I don't mind dealing with the political reporters," Peter said, "but these 'lifestyle' reporters are another thing entirely. Celeste has stopped speaking to any of them."

"Do you have a publicist?" Stone asked.

"The senator has a press officer and an assistant, but they don't work for me."

"If you like, I can recommend a woman

who has been very helpful to clients of mine over the years. She seems to be especially good at making the media go away, or at least, minimizing their presence."

"I'd be grateful for a chance to speak with her."

"I'll e-mail you her particulars tomorrow." Stone looked up to see Alphonse Teppi glide past their table. "Excuse me for a moment, I spy another interloper, a colleague of Ms. Parsons."

Stone's fervent wish was to collar Teppi, take him by the seat of his pants, and haul him to the front door, but discretion in the matter was the better part of valor, and he found another agent and pointed him at the man. The two left the ballroom, arm in arm, appearing to be in the midst of a fascinating conversation. Stone admired the agent's skill in the circumstances. He returned to the table.

"Is all well?" Peter asked.

"Couldn't be better," Stone said. "Tell me, I don't know much about your father, Simon."

"I suppose I could say the same," Peter said. "My parents were divorced when I was quite young, and my father always seemed more like a mysterious uncle, sending a gift about every other birthday or Christmas.

Will has been much more the dad since I was a sprout. I've always thought of him as my real father. The mysterious Simon did me one great favor, though — making me his heir. He came from a line of only sons, so the family fortune wasn't dissipated but handed down intact and very healthy, as you saw when you read my financial statement."

"That was a great gift, since you had a replacement father present in your life."

"I spent a week one summer on Nantucket with him and some cousins from his side of the family, and I was miserable. I felt much more at home on the farm in Georgia, and Grandmother Lee was a real peach."

"Why did you never change your name to Lee?" Stone asked.

"Because Simon would have disinherited me," Peter said, "and Mom wouldn't have that. I'm glad I didn't change it, because the Rule name has provided some shelter over the years from the storm of public interest in the Lee family, as did the years in London, when everybody pretty much forgot about me. Of course, since I've reentered American life and decided to seek office, I'll have to leave that shelter and deal with the world, but at least it will be on my own terms."

"I admire the grip you have on your life,

Peter. When I was thirty I was spending my days solving murders with Dino, and I thought I'd put in my thirty years doing that."

"What changed your mind?"

"A bullet in the knee helped. When Dino and I got involved in a case with some political import, I went my own way and got bounced out of the NYPD for being uncooperative. They used the knee as an excuse."

"You should write an autobiography," Peter said. "Yours sounds like a fascinating life."

The President of the United States, Peter's mother, suddenly appeared between them, and they leaped to their feet.

"Everything going well here?" Kate Lee asked. "Is Peter being a good host?"

"Splendid," Stone said.

"Have a good time," she said, and swept on to the next table.

"I know you've been told this before," Stone said, "but you have a remarkable mother."

"You don't know the half of it," Peter said.

Stone thought he'd like to know the other half, but this didn't seem like the proper occasion.

■ ■ ■ ■

Later, when the party began to die, Stone called Fred and warned him they were on the way outside. As they were getting into the car, Stone looked across the street and saw Gloria Parsons and the lizard Teppi staring at them.

"They're still around?" Holly asked.

"It's funny, a couple of weeks ago I didn't know they existed, and now they seem to be on hand wherever I go."

# 20

On the Monday morning after Thanksgiving, Secretary of State Holly Barker stood on the sidewalk as Fred placed her bags in the trunk of the Bentley.

Stone stood with her. "Would you like Fred for the morning?"

"Thank you, yes. I have a meeting at the UN, and that's my excuse for commandeering an official aircraft for the trip up here. Fred will drop me at the East Side Heliport when I'm done." She hung an arm around his neck and kissed him. "You've been a dear," she said. "I don't know how the weekend could have gone better."

He kissed her back, but he had an idea of how it could have gone better. He waved her off and went back into his office. "Joan," he said, "please get Bob Cantor over here as soon as possible."

"I'm on it," she replied, picking up the

phone.

Bob Cantor was ex-NYPD, an expert on everything technical, now a licensed private investigator of a high order. He was in Stone's office half an hour later, and his van/tech shop was parked at the curb. "What can I do you for, Stone?"

"Bob, there are two people annoying me and friends of mine."

"Shall I use a knife or a gun, or would you prefer to have it look like an accident?"

"It hasn't come to that. Yet. I just want to know everything in their lives that is derogatory and, if possible, illegal."

"What do you suspect them of?"

"For one thing, they're working very hard to get a friend of theirs named Danny Blaine out of Fishkill. It would be very satisfying if they could be caught doing it."

"I know of Blaine — a fashion heartthrob in Fishkill? He must be a very busy young man."

"I expect so. The two people you seek are Gloria Parsons, who is a senior editor at *Just Folks,* and a cohort of hers with no visible means of support named Alphonse Teppi."

"Parsons, I know — or rather, know of. The other one sounds vaguely familiar, but

I can't place him. Where would I find them both?"

"You can find her at or around her magazine, and he will not be far behind. I don't even know where they live."

"And what would you like done to them when I find them?"

"That depends on what you can learn. I don't want violence wrought upon them — I would be content with public disgrace, followed shortly by drawing and quartering."

"So I'll be working in the area of personal destruction, is that it?"

"You don't have to destroy anybody, Bob, and I'm certainly not asking you to do anything illegal. It's just that I've been attacked once by these people, and I feel another one coming on, and I want everything I can get to fight back with. If you could get a nice color close-up of Ms. Parsons being fucked by a donkey, that would be very helpful. Come to think of it, the same goes for Teppi."

"Well, since you put it that way, I don't suppose there's anything in my moral code that would prevent me from helping you publicly humiliate them in a permanent fashion."

"What moral code is that?" Stone asked.

"Exactly. I'll go get 'em. Electronic surveillance okay?"

"As long as you don't get caught doing it."

"Daily reports?"

"Unless you get something sooner or more frequently."

Cantor stood up. "I believe I grasp the scope of my employment. You'll be hearing from me."

"I can't wait."

"Just one thing, Stone."

"What's that?"

"You sound very angry with these people."

"You could say that."

"Someone, I forget who, once said, 'Revenge is a dish best served cold.' Anger can be self-destructive, Stone — be careful."

"You be careful for me, Bob."

"Gotcha," and Bob Cantor left with a little wave.

Stone went back to work with a lighter heart.

Joan buzzed. "Dino on one."

Stone pressed the button. "Good day!"

"You sound happy."

"I feel happy," Stone replied.

"Was that thing last night the bash to end all bashes, or what?"

"I would say it was the bash to end all bashes."

"I don't think I have ever seen a thing of that size carried off with such perfection!"

"How can I disagree with you, Dino?"

"You can't."

"Then I will hold my peace."

"That girl Celeste is the most gorgeous thing I've ever seen. She could do just fine in Hollywood."

"Once again, we are in complete accord."

"And I didn't know that you could serve that much food and drink to that many people and have it turn out so well."

"Once again, accord."

"Although, I think the wine could have used another year."

"Sounds as if you're beginning to have doubts."

"Just another year, maybe two."

"A damning judgment."

"I mean, it was only three years in the bottle."

"Not enough for a very fine Cabernet."

"Do you think so?"

"I'm just agreeing with you."

"Why are you doing that?"

"Because I'm an agreeable guy."

"Not that agreeable — you're up to something."

"You know me too well."

"You sound like a man who is contemplating — no, relishing — revenge upon some unfortunate person."

"That is a very astute judgment."

"I want in on this — c'mon, who is it?"

"All right, it's that horrible woman who said those terrible things about me in that magazine."

"Stone, those were not terrible things. I've told you before, they were complimentary."

"I didn't view them that way."

"What's more, they sounded like they were judgments derived from a certain measure of personal experience."

"I do not care to expand on what I have already said."

"What are you going to do to her?"

"Them."

"You mean Teppi, too?"

"Very likely."

"What do you have on them?"

"I have Bob Cantor on them."

"What has Bob found?"

"He has only just begun."

"Well, if anybody can skewer them, it's Bob. Do you think he can find something I can arrest them for?"

"Please, God."

"You'll keep me posted?"

"With pleasure. Good day, Commissioner." Stone hung up.

# 21

Bob Cantor sat in his idling van, Mozart on the satellite radio, and watched as Gloria Parsons finally left her office building in Soho. He switched off the van and followed on foot for three blocks. Parsons rang a bell at street level, paused for the door to open, then went inside.

Cantor sauntered over to the door and checked the name on the bell: Teppi. Bingo! Two birds possible with one stone! Now all he needed was the right slingshot.

He took a credit-card-sized piece of clear plastic and slipped it into the doorjamb; a moment later the door popped open. Teppi was on the top floor, so Cantor ran lightly up the stairs. It was how he got his exercise. At the top he found an old, steel door wearing too many coats of paint, but it did have a peephole. He removed a small optical instrument from an inside pocket that, when pressed against the peephole, reversed its optical effect, allowing him to get a wide-angle view of Teppi's living room, such as it was.

It was furnished with junk from garage sales and flea markets but still managed to be overdecorated. Parsons and Teppi sat on an old sofa with a blanket over it to hide the tears and cigarette burns in the fabric and sipped coffee from tiny cups. The distance between them supported Cantor's theory about Teppi's sexual persuasion. Parsons was a very nice package, and a straight guy would have already had his hand up her skirt.

Cantor removed a late-nineteenth-century stethoscope about four inches long from another pocket, pressed one end to the door and the other to his ear. The voices from the living room became instantly audible.

"C'mon, Al, what have you got for me?"

"He's straight, good-looking, and rich — all a fella needs in this world to stay in clover and out of trouble. Anyway, you already know a lot more about him than I could ever come up with. I mean, how many times have you fucked him?"

"Several, on two occasions, but that is not relevant to our discussion."

"What, exactly, do you want, Gloria?"

"It doesn't have to be factual, just plausible."

"Now you sound like a politician."

"I didn't come here to be insulted."

"The hell you didn't, you're begging for it. Give me an example of what you're talking about."

"All right, you remember a few years back we did a piece on a guy named . . . well, I've forgotten his name, but his favorite charity was a dog rescue place on the Upper East Side. We managed to insinuate that he was taking two dogs out every day for a walk and having sex with them in the park. I mean, what could the guy say? 'I don't fuck dogs'? Who's going to believe that, once the allegation has been made?"

"You've been inside the guy's house, right, Gloria?"

"I told you, a couple of times."

"Have you ever seen anything so impeccable? It looks like Ralph Lauren personally staged it for a photo shoot. All he needs is a few gorgeous people in tweeds sitting around, a dog or two, and it's perfect!"

"What's your point, Al?"

"All that is a metaphor for the guy's personality. He's squeaky clean!"

"Not in bed, he isn't."

"Just because he visited your every orifice

132

doesn't make him creepy, just enthusiastic."

"I'll grant you his enthusiasm. I need something, and it doesn't have to be sexual."

"Financial, then? I told you, he's rich. I saw a Dun & Bradstreet report on him that was less than three months old, and while he's no billionaire, he's still rolling in it."

"What has he got besides that house?"

"Two houses — he owns the one next door, too. The butler, cook, and secretary all live there."

"What else?"

"A house in Paris and a country estate in England. A summer place in Maine, too."

"You're depressing me, Al."

"Gloria, instead of trying to torpedo the guy, you should be trying to marry, then divorce him. That's how a girl gets ahead in this city, if she's not a tech wizard or a CEO."

"That's sexist, Al."

"Maybe. I'm an equal opportunity sexist — I go both ways when it comes to marrying money."

"Al, you just gave me an idea. Can you get me a copy of that D&B you saw?"

"Yeah, but it'll cost."

"How much?"

"That's inside stuff, unless you're a bank. Say, five hundred? Two hundred now."

She reached for her purse, fished out two bills, and handed them over.

"What have you got in mind, Gloria?"

"Well, we already know that the bulk of his fortune came from his dead wife, and before that, from her first husband, the movie star Vance Calder."

"That's been published, sweetie, along with the details of her murder."

"Maybe, but it hasn't been mined for dirt."

"What you need is *pay* dirt."

"Where there's enough money, there's plenty of pay dirt."

"What does it matter who he inherits from? An old man or an old lady — what's the dif?"

"It's *sexy* money, rooted in the movies. What's sexier than Hollywood? Let's start with who Vance Calder screwed to get it."

"Okay, I can plow that field. Give me a week."

"You can have three days." Gloria stood up, smoothed her skirt, checked her hair in a gigantic mirror across the room, and headed for the door. "Oh, and one other thing, Al. Check out his wife's murder and see if there are any holes in the story."

"Whatever you say."

Outside, Cantor looked around. Upstairs

or down? He slipped out of his loafers, tucked them under an arm, went for up, the stairs leading to the roof. He had just crouched at the top when Parsons burst through Teppi's door and started down the stairs, apparently unwilling to wait for the elevator. Cantor noticed that the phone box was there, and he quickly attached a remote device that would record any conversations in his van. Then he went after Parsons, got to the front door, and looked up and down the street to see her stopping at a shop window, then disappearing inside.

He started toward the shop, taking his time, window-shopping, using reflections to keep an eye on the door. He was nearly there when she emerged, carrying a tiny shopping bag. Cosmetics, he guessed.

She walked back to her office building and went inside.

Cantor figured the place to start on her would be in the pieces she had written. He found a coffee shop, ordered a pastry and a double espresso, and went to work on his extra-large iPhone, trolling for celebrity peccadilloes and journalistic outrages.

## 22

Alphonse Teppi sat in his corner computer station and Googled "Barrington Murder." Instantly, he got acres of stuff from newspapers in New York and Virginia, where the murder took place.

The place was Arrington Calder Barrington's recently completed country house in Albemarle County; there were four pages of photos in *Architectural Digest* showing nearly every part of the house, including the large downstairs foyer where the woman had been killed with a shotgun, allegedly by a former lover, an architecture professor at the University of Virginia named Rutherford.

He looked for details that were less architectural and more lascivious, and he found what he was looking for in a local Virginia newspaper, including a reconstruction of the crime scene. Barrington couldn't have had anything to do with it because he had been out riding with his and Arrington's son and the boy's girlfriend, and they had all heard the shotgun go off from the stables, where they had just arrived. There was one loose end, though — the ex-boyfriend and alleged murderer had fled the scene and the state, and he had finally been shot in the head in Barrington's office by Joan Robertson, his secretary. The dead man had never been charged with Arrington's murder, and he told friends that he had been falsely accused and that the husband had done it. An idea began forming in Teppi's fevered imagination. He called Gloria.

"That was fast," she said.

"My brain got lucky," Teppi replied. He recounted the details of the murder to her.

"Yeah, that's about the way I remember it," Parsons said.

"Do you remember that the alleged murderer, this guy named Rutherford, went to Stone Barrington's office with a gun, ostensibly to kill Barrington, and for his trouble got shot in the head by Barrington's secretary?"

"Well, yeah, I think I remember that."

"Thus closing the case?"

"The guy is dead — they could hardly prosecute him."

"But there's your opening," Teppi explained. "Officially the murder case against him was never adjudicated. What if what he told his friends was true? That he didn't shoot Arrington, that Barrington was persecuting him."

"So, you mean that Barrington could have killed his wife?"

"The important words are 'could have.' "

"But he had an alibi — he was with his son and the kid's girlfriend in the stables when they all heard the gun go off."

"They heard something that *sounded* like a gun. In fact, Barrington told the police that it sounded like a door slamming. And there was no one else in the house."

"So, how could Barrington have killed her?"

"Maybe he shot her before they went riding, or something like that. It doesn't really matter, all you want to do is to call Barrington's story and the police report into question. Nobody actually saw Rutherford in the house at the time, and the police never got to question him because he scampered."

"But the local cops would see that she was shot at the time Barrington said she was. The physical evidence, like body temperature, would have told them that."

"Yeah, but it's a Podunk sheriff's office in rural Virginia. Can you imagine how many ways they could have screwed up the physical evidence? Don't you remember how Johnnie Cochran took apart the LAPD at the O.J. trial? And that was a big-city, lotsa-science police department."

"Jesus, Al," Parsons said, "I believe you're actually on to something."

"Well, I mean, they're not going to arrest Barrington for the murder, but there'll be a lot of press, and half the people who read it will remember only that Barrington *could* have done it. Do I have to explain to *you* how the public thinks?"

"No, Al, you don't," Parsons said. "I'm going to have a word with my editor."

"And don't forget, you owe me another three hundred."

"Al, the five hundred was for the D&B report."

"Picky, picky, picky!"

"Okay, if this story flies with my editor, you'll get the other three hundred."

Gloria sat in her editor's office, a hip slung on the woman's desk. "What do you think?"

"I think what I thought at the time," the editor said, "that Barrington had nothing to do with his wife's murder, that Rutherford did it."

"Hazel," Parsons said, "how do you *know* that?"

"Well, I don't know it, it's just what the police and everybody said at the time."

"A Podunk sheriff's office in rural Virginia — they could have screwed up the physical evidence a hundred ways. Don't you remember the O.J. trial? The prosecution had him on the physical evidence, then Johnnie Cochran shredded their handling of the blood!"

"You'd have to handle this very, very carefully, Gloria."

"Listen, I'm never going to say outright that Barrington murdered his wife, I'm just asking the questions that the public will demand be answered."

Hazel looked at her appraisingly. "Gloria, tell me the truth, did you fuck Barrington?"

"What's that got to do with anything?"

"Have you got some sort of ax to grind here? Did he dump you, or something?"

"Hazel, if I answered that question, you'd have every right to fire me for being too forthcoming. I'll answer your first question, though. Did I fuck Barrington? Yes, I did, and it was great! But by the time anybody who reads my story gets around to asking that question, my work will be done. Half the world will think that Barrington *could*

140

have murdered his wife."

"Just like O.J.," Hazel mused. "Okay, do a first draft, and we'll go over it together word by word."

"You'll have it tomorrow morning," Parsons said. She went back to her office, fired up her computer, and wrote with abandon, spinning out her story, innuendo by innuendo, and finishing with one short paragraph: "Is Arrington Calder Barrington's murderer still on the loose? And if so, who might he be?"

She printed the story and sprinted down the hallway to her editor's office.

Hazel looked up at her. "Already?"

"You said you wanted to see a first draft. Here it is." She slapped the pages on the desk.

The editor read through the manuscript slowly, making an occasional mark with a grease pencil.

"Well?"

"Here," Hazel said, "address the places I've marked, being sure that any insinuations we make are justified."

Parsons looked over the story quickly. "That's it? That's all that worries you?"

"That's it."

"Tell you what, we'll license the *Architectural Digest* photos and splash them all over the story, including the murder spot."

"That's a brilliant idea, Gloria, it will give our readers just the verisimilitude they need to draw just the conclusion we want them to. Also, see if you can get crime-scene photos from the Virginia cops, and talk to the investigating officer, too." She picked up the phone. "I'll get the lawyers in here right away. You clean up the manuscript and we'll feed it to them, page by page, and get an opinion."

"I'm on it!" Parsons cried, and ran back to her office. "Hazel," she said under her breath to herself, "before a year has passed, I'll have winnowed you out of your job, and I'll use this story to do it!"

# 23

Sitting in the coffee shop, Bob Cantor used his iPhone to do searches on Gloria Parsons and Alphonse Teppi. He found no criminal charges or arrests, but Teppi had been questioned many times by the police. There had been two libel suits filed against Parsons and her magazine, *Just Folks,* but both had been settled out of court. He paid his bill and went back to his van, but he didn't think to check his automatic recorder. The red light glowed entertainingly behind his head, but he just didn't notice.

Gloria got the Virginia sheriff on the line; she was surprised that he had so readily taken her call. "Sheriff?"

"Sheriff Rudolf Sweat," he replied.

"Sheriff Sweat, this is Gloria Parsons from *Just Folks* magazine."

"Oh, yeah, Gloria, I know your stuff."

"I'm so pleased to have a reader in Albemarle County."

"You got lotsa readers down here."

"Thank you so much. May I call you Rudy?"

"Nobody else does, but you can."

"Do you mind if I record our conversation, so I won't misquote you?"

"You go right ahead."

Gloria switched on the recorder. "Were you the investigating officer on the Arrington Calder Barrington murder?"

"I was one of 'em. Old Sheriff Bates took the lead on everything, until I beat him at the polls last election."

"Well, congratulations, Rudy."

"Thank you, Gloria. Like I was saying, I was on the scene the whole time, first officer present, in fact. Sheriff Bates got there half an hour later."

"And what did you find?"

"Dead woman, shotgun to the back of the head. It was a mess."

"Did you follow crime-scene procedure after that?" Gloria asked.

"Crime-scene procedure around here at the time was to wait for Sheriff Bates to get there and don't let nobody touch nothing."

"Tell me what happened from the beginning."

"Well, Mr. Barrington called nine-one-one

and got transferred to us. I was in a radio car a few miles off, and I took the call. The sheriff was in Charlottesville, and it took him a lot longer."

"What did you do in the meantime?"

"I taped off the scene and got Barrington and the two kids into the library and started asking questions."

"Did you like the answers?"

"They seemed right to me, and the three of them had the same story. Wait a minute, there was some difference. The kids had taken their saddles into the tack room, and Barrington heard the gunshot while they were gone, I think."

"Then what?"

"Then they went up to the house, found the front door open and Mrs. Barrington there, dead."

"Was there a lot of blood?"

"Blood and brains — it was a shotgun."

"Did you form an opinion about when the gunshot was heard?"

"Yeah, less than five minutes before Barrington got there."

"Let me ask you, Rudy, is it possible that the gunshot came earlier than that?"

"How do you mean?"

"Well, Barrington was the only one who heard it. Could he have been wrong?"

"I think I see where you're going, here, Gloria. You mean he might have just made up hearing it?"

"Is that possible?"

"Well, anything's possible, I guess."

"Suppose you had evidence that somebody else heard the gunshot earlier?"

"Wasn't nobody else in the house when I got there."

"What happened when Sheriff Bates got there?"

"He started all over — that was his way, he didn't trust nobody else."

"Did he get the same answers?"

"Yep."

"And did he accept them as true?"

"I guess. He did spend some time with Barrington on what he heard and when he heard it."

"Tell me — this is just hypothetical — while the kids were in the tack room was there time for Barrington to go up to the house, shoot his wife, hide the shotgun, and come back to the stable before the kids came out of the tack room?"

"Well, that's hard to say. I didn't write down no timeline, and neither did the sheriff. I guess we just both thought the murderer had come and gone. There might have been time for Barrington to do that, though."

"How did you settle on Rutherford as the murderer?"

"Barrington suggested him, said he had been bothering his wife for several days, calling her up and the like."

"Did you consider anyone else?"

"Well, no, we had eliminated Barrington, and there wasn't another person who had had contact with her in the days before. Also, Rutherford ran. He was out of his house and gone by the time we got there. Why else would he have ran if he wasn't guilty?"

"How did Stone Barrington act while you were there?"

"He was stunned, sort of, and then he was quiet and calm — I think he wanted to keep the kids quiet and calm, too."

"He wanted to keep them quiet?"

"Yeah. He talked to them a little bit and then left them in the library while he came out and talked to the sheriff and me."

"What was his reaction to the dead body in the hall?"

"I'd say, kind of clinical, professional. I heard later he used to be a police officer in New York. I guess it wasn't his first shotgun to the head. Come to think of it, he did better than I did."

"How long were you and the sheriff at the crime scene?"

"Must have been a couple of hours. We had to wait for some people to come from the hospital and look at the body and do what they had to do."

"Were blood samples taken?"

"I expect so, but since we never needed them for a trial, they didn't seem so important. By the time we left, the body was gone, and the servants were cleaning up the mess."

"Who asked the servants to do that?"

"Mr. Barrington did. I couldn't blame him, and the sheriff told him to go ahead."

"Rudy, a personal question — did you ever, at any time, consider that Barrington might have been the killer, instead of Rutherford?"

"No, but the sheriff did — we talked about it."

"And what was his opinion?"

"He thought we ought to keep an open mind until we had found Rutherford and questioned him. He was like that, real thorough."

"Rudy, how can I get in touch with Sheriff Bates? I'd like to talk to him."

"You can't. He had a heart attack when he heard about the election results and died on the way to the hospital."

"Do you know if he made any statements about the Barrington murder before he died?"

"No, I wasn't there when he collapsed. I went to the hospital, but like I said, he had died on the way."

"Rudy, thank you so much. Can I call you again if I have any further questions?"

"Sure, Gloria, anytime at all. If you want to come down here and look around, I'll be glad to escort you."

She thanked him again and hung up. She had enough.

# 24

Gloria Parsons switched on her computer, pulled up her first draft on the Barrington murder, and began going through it, line by line, inserting fragments of her interview with Sheriff Rudolf Sweat. Half an hour into the piece she called Hazel Schwartz, her boss, and said, "Hazel, I'll be ready for the lawyers in fifteen minutes."

"I'll have them here," Hazel said.

Parsons finished her piece, spell-checked it, printed four copies, and walked down the hall to Hazel's corner office. Two lawyers, Jim and Martina, were just sitting down. Parsons distributed the copies to her boss and the lawyers and waited while they read it.

Jim looked up. "This looks pretty clean to me. Are these quotes with the yokel cop accurate?"

"I have him on tape," Parsons replied.

"I've got a couple of nitpicks," Martina

said. She brought up her points and Parsons made the changes on the spot. "I'll put in the corrections and e-mail them to you in ten minutes," she said.

Hazel spoke up. "I got the *Architectural Digest* photos licensed. An art director is working on the layout now. We'll go over it together when he's done." She gave Parsons his e-mail address. "Forward it to him, and he'll have full-blown comp ready for us to review."

Parsons went back to her office, and in ten minutes she was done, and, she reckoned, so was Stone Barrington. She went back to Hazel's office, and they went over the layout on her giant computer screen that could show half a dozen pages at once.

They settled on a headline:

## COULD THE BARRINGTON MURDERER BE BARRINGTON?

"Love it," Hazel said. "Gloria, I'm giving you a two-hundred-dollar-a-week raise, effective next pay period."

"Thank you, Hazel," Parsons gushed. She had expected a five-hundred-dollar raise, but she could lie in wait for a while longer. She left Hazel's office whistling a little tune.

There was a cocktail party uptown that

she had been thinking of passing on, but she was thirsty and horny, and one never knew who would be there, did one? She phoned for an Uber, and did her makeup in the backseat on the way.

The party had been under way for an hour when she got there, and it was more elegant than she had imagined. The apartment was on Fifth Avenue and had a low-floor view of the park, like a close-up, and the people were well dressed. Then she looked across the room to a corner bar and there, all alone and looking depressed, was the governor of the State of New York, one Benton Blake. She made a beeline for the bar and set herself on a stool right in front of him, not bothering to pull her skirt down. She was wearing a black Armani suit and a silk blouse that showed an impressive amount of her creamy breasts, and his eyes went directly there, just as they were supposed to.

"Hi, there," he said, offering his hand. "I'm Benton. Who are you?"

"I'm Gloria," she said; she didn't want to mention her last name, in case he recognized it and got cautious. She squeezed his hand for a second longer than he had expected. "And I'd like a very dry vodka martini."

"Certainly," he said.

"Will you join me?"

"Of course." He ordered from the bartender and held up two fingers.

Parsons reviewed what she knew about him: his wife had left him two weeks ago for another man, a real estate developer. It wasn't public yet, but Parsons knew a few details. The wife had pretty much moved into the man's penthouse, and Governor Blake wouldn't speak her name to his staff. The man was tall, slim, and fit, and once he started to recover, he would have the ladies lined up and waiting. Parsons decided to accelerate his recovery.

She accepted her martini, raised her glass to him while locking in on his eyes, and took a man-sized gulp. He followed suit.

"There," he said.

"Is everything all better now?" she asked, licking the vodka from her lips.

"I'm getting there," he said.

"What can I do to help?"

"That's a leading question," he replied.

They both took another gulp of martini.

"Then lead on," Gloria said.

"Where would you like to be led?"

"All the way past my better judgment," she replied.

That got a good laugh. "It sounds like an

inviting place," he said. "Where would we find it? Your place?"

"That's way downtown," she said, "and I don't think I can wait that long." She ran a fingernail from his knee up his inner thigh. "Isn't there a bedroom in this apartment?"

"Well, let's see," he said. "The one with the coats is right over there, but that doesn't offer much privacy. On the other hand, there's another just beyond it that's much better."

"Does it have a lock on the door?" she asked.

"If it doesn't, we can jury-rig something."

"You go ahead, I'll be sixty seconds behind you," she said, downing what was left of her martini.

He did the same, turned and walked away. Gloria consulted her watch, then followed. The door was slightly ajar, and she went in and closed it behind her. She leaned on the door and kicked off her Manolos, then slipped off her suit jacket and hung it on the doorknob.

Blake was sitting on the bed, leaning back on his hands, watching. His coat was already off, and he loosened his tie. She strolled across the bedroom toward him, unbuttoning her blouse and unhooking her bra from the front. She put her hand under his chin and kissed him, using her tongue to good effect, and dropped her handbag on the bed.

He took a breast in his hand and pinched the nipple lightly.

"You've just found the hot button," she said. "Where's yours?"

He pulled her gently to her knees, and she could see the growing bulge under his trousers. "You're getting warm," he said.

She unzipped his trousers, liberated a very attractive penis, and kissed it a few times, while he made appreciative noises. "Before we go any further, there's something I want," she said, caressing him with a hand.

"You don't look like that kind of a girl," he said.

"Thank you, I'm not."

"Then tell me what I can do for you," he said, breathing faster.

"I have a young friend who is doing three years at Fishkill," she said, "for a crime he didn't commit. He's being, ah, abused daily by other inmates."

"And how can I help your friend? I can't do a pardon."

"Just commute his sentence to time served, for exigent family reasons."

"Done," he said.

She reached into her purse and produced her little recorder. "Repeat after me," she said. "I, Benton Blake, in return for the best sex of my life . . ."

He repeated.

". . . do promise to commute the sentence of Daniel Blaine to time served . . ."

He repeated.

"Within forty-eight hours of this time." She recited the date and time.

He completed his promise. "Now come here," he said.

She dropped the recorder into her purse, stripped him, then returned to her original work.

Over the next hour and a half she brought him off, then again, then got started on a third performance before he begged her to stop.

"I'll give you the other half of that when Danny Blaine is a free man," she said.

"It will be done tomorrow," he breathed. "I'll want you again tomorrow night." He fished a card from his trousers pocket. "The cell number is there."

She found a card of her own. "Eight o'clock at my place," she said. "We'll order in and make a night of it."

# 25

Gloria was getting out of the shower at ten o'clock the following morning when her cell phone went off.

"It's Gloria," she said into it.

"Sweetheart," Danny said, "I don't know how you managed it, but I'm getting out of here at one today. Can you pick me up?"

"You betcha," she said, and hung up.

Gloria fixed herself up and repatriated her car from the garage around the corner. The drive took an hour and a half, with traffic, and she was five minutes early; five minutes later, Danny was let out of a small door in a big door by a uniformed guard, who handed him an envelope and shook his hand.

She got out of the car to greet him with a big hug. "You've lost weight," she said.

"I've had more exercise than usual," he replied.

"I hope you weren't getting to like it, that

would be a great loss to the women of New York."

"No, I wasn't, but I was getting used to it. I'm never getting into a shower again unless I'm alone and the bathroom door is locked."

"I've been paying the rent on your place," she said. "We'll go straight there."

"No, not there," he said.

"Where, then?"

"McDonald's."

"There's one before we get to the interstate," she said.

"I can taste it already. If I ever get sent to prison again, I want you to shoot me as soon as my sentence is pronounced."

"I'll keep that in mind."

"How did you spring me?"

"I happened to meet Governor Blake at a party last night," she said. "We got along."

"Oh, the magic you do with your body," he said, laughing.

"The fun wasn't all his. He's a very attractive man, and I'm seeing him again tonight."

"You mean we can't have dinner?"

"You have a long list of girls to work your way through," she said, digging an envelope out of her bag and handing it to him. "I stopped at an ATM on the way."

"You think of everything."

"Tomorrow, you can start thinking of everything for yourself — it'll be fun. I made a couple of calls, and you've got an interview at ten am tomorrow at *W,* with the Style editor. She's going to love you." She gave him a slip of paper with the name and address. "You'll be at work again by noon."

"That's great," Danny said. "Now what can I do for you?"

"Well, there was somebody I wanted you to murder, but I think I've pretty well taken care of that myself. Read the new issue, it's on the stands in a couple of days."

"I pity the poor guy. What did he do to you?"

"He was rude," she said.

Gloria looked out the window and saw Benton Blake arrive downstairs, his black car followed by a State Police SUV. The two vehicles rolled away, leaving him on the sidewalk. Her bell rang a moment later.

"Top floor," she said into the intercom.

"On my way."

She let him in, and he had a good look around. "I like your style," he said, "and I like the views."

"Drink?"

"Do you have any single-malt scotch?"

She gave him a choice of three labels; he

accepted one over ice, and she poured herself one. "Hungry?"

"Starved."

"You like Chinese?"

"I like good Chinese."

"I'll give you great Chinese."

"Is that a technique?"

"Yes, but that's later." She phoned in an order, then sat down beside him on the sofa. "Thank you for what you did for Danny," she said. "He's home safe."

"I do only one get-out-of-jail-free card, so don't ask me again."

"I promise I won't."

"Something else — I didn't know your last name or where you worked until I looked at your card. Don't ever mention my name or refer to my office in your magazine."

"What if it's favorable?"

"In my experience, what's favorable to one is a nightmare to another. Take Stone Barrington, for instance."

"You know Stone Barrington?"

"He was a year ahead of me in law school, and he's a reliable and generous contributor. I haven't spoken to him, but I don't think he would have liked what you said about him in your piece about Holly Barker."

"I thought it complimentary."

160

"Stone would think it extremely embarrassing. He's not a part of the media culture — at least, not until your piece — and he's unaccustomed to being handled that way."

"Apologize to him for me when you see him again."

"I don't think I'll bring it up."

The doorbell rang, and she buzzed up the deliveryman. She spread half a dozen cartons on the dining table and got silver and napkins placed. "Dinner's on," she said.

He sat down and began serving himself, while she opened a bottle of Chardonnay. "You were right," he said, tasting a couple of dishes, "this is great Chinese."

"They're practically next door."

"Lucky you. I don't do so well in Albany."

"Do you spend much time in the city?"

"I have a place here." He looked at her over a forkful of lo mein. "And I'm thinking about not running again." He thought for a moment. "I haven't mentioned that to anyone else, so if I see it in print, I'll know how it got there."

"You've already made your point," she said. "I have a very good lock on my lips when I'm not using them for something else."

He smiled and chewed at the same time.

"I was looking out the window when you

161

got here. You arrived stylishly."

"I could hardly take the subway," he said, "and cabdrivers have magazines like yours on speed dial. Anyway, the State Police are very protective of me, not to mention discreet. It's a nice way to travel, and I'll miss it. And the helicopter."

"You have your own helicopter?"

"Every governor in the country has a chopper," he said. "Why do you think they run for the office?"

"More wine?" she asked.

"More you," he said, reaching for her.

He got what he wanted, and more.

## 26

Stone called the best publicist in town, Faith Mackey, and was put through immediately.

"Good morning, Faith."

"Good morning, Stone. I was about to call you."

"About what?"

"You, first."

"I have a potential client for you."

"Oh, goody!"

"And everything I say about him from here on stops with you."

"That's always understood, dear."

"His name is Peter Rule."

"Why does that ring a bell?"

"Faith, I'm disappointed in you — he's the son of the President of the United States." He could hear her palm smacking her forehead.

"Stupid me. He just got married, right? What does he need?"

"Here's the story in a nutshell. He's her son by her first marriage, to a high CIA official. He's thirty years old. He attended Princeton and Harvard, was a Rhodes Scholar, and spent some years in London working in finance. He came back four years ago and went to work in Eliot Saltonstall's Senate office. He's going to run for the other New York seat in two years. After that, the sky's the limit."

"Who was the publicist for the Metropolitan Club?"

"The White House."

"That explains why they didn't call me."

"Peter is calling you now. From here on in he's going to need very sensitive handling. I'm told he knows every elected official in New York State, but the public is pretty much unaware of him. The wedding dinner was the kickoff for his relationship with the voters."

"Got it."

"He's a young man with a very clean nose, not even a DUI — I know, I checked. He's inherited old money from his father, Simon Rule, who died a couple of years ago. He's got houses in Georgetown and the Hamptons and an apartment in New York."

"I need addresses and phone numbers."

"Get them from him. I e-mailed him your

contact information ten minutes ago."

"Got it. I'll make him famous in stages — famous for what, he and I have to talk about."

"He's got a gorgeous new wife. That's a start."

"I thank you, Stone."

"All right, why were you going to call me?"

"Not good news. I just got proofs of a piece in *Just Folks,* by that awful slut Gloria Parsons."

"What is it this time?"

"She's practically accusing you of murdering your wife."

*"What?"*

"I'm not kidding, Stone, this is serious. She knows it's not true, she knows she can't prove it, but the rub-off from this could follow you for the rest of your life if it's not handled right. I'd like to help."

"What should I do?"

"You're a lawyer — file a libel suit and ask a judge for an injunction to stop publication. That will scare the shit out of them, because by tomorrow it will have gone to press and it would cost them a ton of money to stop press, excise the story, and reprint. You'd better have a summons in their hands before noon. They've already sent proofs to tastemakers, people like me, and that will be damaging enough."

"Can you e-mail me the proofs?"

"Sure I can. I should start writing a press release about your lawsuit, and it should hit the street seconds after you've served them. You're the lawyer, but I suggest you name Gloria Parsons and her editor, Hazel Schwartz, in your suit. That will make them think about being personally liable, even after their lawyers tell them you can't make it stick. You or your lawyer should also write an account of the circumstances surrounding the crime that can go out with my release and give the press something to quote. Include the names of any law enforcement people involved so that they can be called for statements. Shall we get started?"

"You're damned right," Stone said. "I'll shoot you the account of the crime as reported by the *New York Times.* That pretty much covered everything."

"I can dig that out myself from their website," Faith said. "Get your lawsuit in gear." She hung up.

Stone called Herbie Fisher, his protégé partner at Woodman & Weld, and explained the situation.

"I can dig up some libel boilerplate, fill in the names, and have them served in an

166

hour," Herbie said. "How much do you want to sue for?"

"I don't know, a hundred million?"

"The magazine is owned by something called Fastbuck Publications, which is, in turn, owned by some conglomerate. I can't remember which one, but I'll find out and I'll have them served simultaneously."

"Go!"

Joan buzzed. "Dino on one."

Stone pressed the button. "Hey."

"Hey, dinner tonight? Patroon at seven-thirty?"

"Sure, but I've gotta go right now. *Just Folks* magazine is running a piece saying that I killed Arrington."

"That's horseshit," Dino said.

"I know that, you know that, but now I have to let the world know it."

"See you at seven-thirty, if you haven't left the country." Dino hung up.

Stone got on his computer, found the *Times* stories, printed them out, and read them. He was grateful to the newspaper of record for having been so thorough.

He heard a text come in: it was from Herbie: *Fastbuck Publications is owned by St. Clair Enterprises. That ring a bell?*

It certainly did; Stone, Mike Freeman, and Charley Fox, or Triangle Partnership, as they were known, had set up their company for the express purpose of buying all the assets of St. Clair Enterprises. He called Charley Fox.

"Hey, Stone, what's up?"

"We own all the assets of St. Clair Enterprises, don't we?"

"We do, lock, stock, and belt buckle."

"Does that include a company called Fastbuck Publications?"

"Hang on, I'll see." There was heard the tapping of keys on a computer keyboard. "It does, and what do you know, I've got a get-acquainted lunch with their CEO this very day, name of Alfred Finch."

"Holy shit, Charley," he said. "There's something I'd like you to hand to Mr. Finch when you meet him."

"What's that?"

"A libel suit." Stone went on to explain, and they made a plan.

# 27

Alfred Finch sat in his hotel room and read the Stone Barrington piece. He loved it. They would get huge mileage out of this — thousands of e-mails to the editors, pro and con, and Barrington would probably sue; the story would live for months, maybe years. He e-mailed both Hazel Schwartz and Gloria Parsons and approved the raise for Parsons, adding another hundred dollars a week.

Fastbuck Publications was located in a small Florida town where the rents, taxes, and printing costs were reasonable. *Just Folks* had been growing apace since its introduction four years before, and circulation was running close to three million. Christian St. Clair had bought the magazine at the beginning of its second year, and when he had died, Finch feared he'd get a new owner who wouldn't allow him to sail so close to the wind with his editorial policy, which was pretty much Anything Goes, unless it involved losing a libel suit, which had never happened. He wouldn't lose a Barrington suit, either; he was confident of it.

Finch had flown to New York for the single purpose of meeting Charles Fox, CEO of the investment group that had bought all of St. Clair's assets, and he had put together a winning summary of the publication's progress during the past three years. He planned to come out of this lunch meeting with a free editorial hand.

While in the city, in addition to meeting Fox, he planned to visit the editorial offices of *Just Folks,* in SoHo, see *Hamilton,* and, maybe, get laid. He'd had his eye on Gloria Parsons since they'd hired her, and they were having dinner that evening. His expectations were high.

His lunch with his new boss was at St. Clair's old headquarters in the East Sixties, which he'd seen only from a passing cab; he was looking forward to seeing the interior. He grabbed a cab uptown and arrived at the stroke of one o'clock.

Once there, he climbed a curving marble staircase to Fox's office and was met by a secretary. "Please have a seat, Mr. Finch," she said, pointing him at a leather sofa. "Mr. Fox is on a phone call with one of his investment partners and shouldn't be much longer."

Finch settled into the sofa and picked up a copy of *Town & Country* from the coffee table and leafed through it. He was happy that he didn't have to deal with the class of stiffs that the publication covered, or at least, from their point of view. He'd rather be nipping at the upper crust's asses from below the waterline, like the shark he imagined himself to be.

The secretary's phone buzzed. She spoke into it, then rose. "Right this way, Mr. Finch," she said, walking to the ornate double doors nearby. She opened one and said, "Mr. Fox, Mr. Alfred Finch is here."

"Send him in," a voice echoed from the big room.

As the door opened, Finch could see a table set for two on one side of the room, which was, in fact, a library containing thousands of volumes. A surprisingly young man sat at a large table before a carved marble fireplace. "Come in, Alfred," he said.

"It's Al," Finch said, taking the extended hand.

"And I'm Charley," Fox said. "Have you been here before?"

"First time I've been inside," Finch said.

"Was this Christian St. Clair's personal library?"

"Yes, with every book he loved beautifully bound," Charley said, making a sweeping motion with his hand. "Nearly five thousand volumes on two decks." A spiral staircase led to a mezzanine with still more bookcases.

"Shall we sit down? Lunch is on its way up from the kitchen downstairs."

"Certainly," Finch replied, happy at the warmth of his reception. Charley Fox must have been doing his homework, reading the weekly reports he'd sent up from Florida. Finch was being made to feel right at home in this imposing mansion.

The two men sat down, and a waitress appeared through a hidden door with a bottle of champagne — Dom Pérignon, Finch noted, not the cheap stuff. She poured some for Fox to taste; he did so, then she poured two glasses. It went down wonderfully well.

"Have you been reading my weeklies?" he asked.

"Your reports or your magazine?"

"Hopefully both."

"I've certainly been reading your reports. My taste in magazines doesn't include *Just Folks.*"

"Well, I don't love everything we publish,

myself, but it's all grist for our particular mill, and our audience is constantly growing."

"Of course," Fox said. "I understand you have to publish to the popular tastes."

"I'm glad you do, it saves me from making that particular sales pitch. Christian St. Clair had a little trouble dealing with it in the beginning, but as our circulation grew, he came to understand the business we're in."

The waitress came in with a cream soup, and they started to eat.

"I'm thinking of shutting down *Just Folks,*" Fox said.

Finch thought he hadn't heard him correctly. "How's that again?"

"I'm thinking of shutting down your magazine."

Finch put down his soup spoon and took a gulp of his champagne. "I'm sorry, I don't understand you — you said you've been reading my weekly reports."

"Yes, and for the first time I took a good look at the magazine," Fox said. "In fact, I found an article which mentioned an acquaintance of mine in rather an unseemly light."

"Which piece was that?" Finch said, fighting to keep his breathing under control.

"The article about our new secretary of state, Holly Barker, which featured a photograph of a gentleman named Stone Barrington."

"I thought the piece mentioned him favorably," Finch stammered.

"Oddly, Mr. Barrington didn't see it that way. In fact, he was very embarrassed by the reference to him."

"I'm very sorry to hear that," Finch said. "I'll be very happy to instruct the editor to issue a fulsome apology, if you think that might make Mr. Barrington feel better."

There was a pause while Fox took a sip of his champagne. "I understand you have an article about Mr. Barrington in your upcoming issue," Fox said.

"That is correct," Finch said. "Is there some problem with the piece?"

"The problem is, it practically accuses the man of murdering his wife."

"Well, the piece never quite says that," Finch said. "In fact, our lawyers have approved it with hardly any changes."

"Al, surely you know who owns your magazine now."

"Why, of course, it's Triangle Partnership, isn't it?"

"Do you know who represents the corners of the triangle?"

"Well, I assume you are one."

"That's correct. Another is Michael Freeman, the CEO of Strategic Services, the security company."

"Ah, big outfit."

"Yes, indeed. And do you know who is the third corner of Triangle Partnership?"

"No," Finch said weakly, but he was beginning to suspect.

"Our third partner is Stone Barrington," Fox said.

"Oh, my God," Finch muttered, wiping beads of sweat from his forehead.

"God cannot help you now," Fox said. "Now, I want you to follow my instructions precisely."

# 28

Charley Fox looked across the table at the sweating man opposite him. "Do you have a cell phone?" he asked.

"Yes, of course," Finch replied, mopping his face with his linen napkin.

"Then I want you to call the New York offices of *Just Folks* and speak to the editor, Hazel Schwartz. I want you to instruct her to stop the presses, if they have already started, then to excise the Barrington piece from the new issue and substitute something else. Do you understand me?"

"Yes, sir," Finch replied. He set the phone on the table and dialed the office number.

"Put it on speaker so I can hear both sides of the conversation," Charley said.

Finch pressed the speaker button.

"Oh, and fire Gloria Parsons. Tell her if she isn't out of the building with her personal effects in fifteen minutes, Security will come and throw her bodily out of the building, preferably out of a window."

"Yes, sir." There goes getting laid tonight, Finch thought to himself. The number was ringing.

Hazel Schwartz and Gloria Parsons sat in the editor's office, sipping from their own bottle of Dom Pérignon.

"I can't wait for the fuss to start," Hazel said. "This is going to be such fun."

Hazel didn't have long to wait for the fuss to start; her phone rang. She pressed the speaker button. "This is Hazel."

"Hazel, this is Al Finch."

"Good afternoon, Al," Hazel said. "We just went to press with the new issue."

"Hazel," he said, "stop the presses."

"What is this, a game?"

"Stop the presses."

"Al, do you know what it would cost to stop the presses, then start them again?"

"Hazel!" Finch shouted. "Stop the fucking presses!"

"All right, Al, I'll call them immediately."

"Replace the Barrington piece with something else, then restart."

"Al, if your problem is the Barrington piece, the lawyers have already vetted it within an inch of its life. It's fine."

"Replace the goddamned Barrington piece!"

"I'm calling right now, on another line." Hazel picked up her cell phone and called the printers. She asked if the issue had gone to press and was told it had. "Stop the presses," she said, being sure that Finch could hear her. "I said stop the presses! We'll reformat the issue and get back to you in an hour or so." She hung up. "There, Al, did you hear that? I stopped the presses."

Across her desk, Gloria was mouthing, "What's wrong?"

"I heard you, Hazel. Now call Gloria Parsons into your office and fire her, effective immediately."

"What?"

"If she isn't out of the building in fifteen minutes, call Security and have her thrown out."

"I get it, Al, I'll speak to her immediately."

"Call me back on my cell when it's done, and tell me what you're substituting for the Barrington piece."

"I will, Al." Hazel hung up.

Gloria exploded. "What the fuck is going on? He just upped my raise to three hundred!"

"You heard him, it's all about the Barrington piece."

"Barrington must have gotten to Al some-how. How did he do that?"

"How should I know? Anyway, you heard Al — you'd better clear out your office and get out before I call him back. I'll call you later, when I've found out what's going on."

Gloria stormed out of the office, swearing, and went to her office.

Hazel got on her computer, found a piece they had pulled from the magazine about a movie star, and copied it into the master. When she had confirmed that the substitution was seamless and that the cover tease on Barrington was gone, she pressed the send key, and it went to the printer. She called Al Finch back.

Finch pressed the button on his cell phone; he was still on speaker. "Hazel?"

"Yes, Al, it's done. I've pulled the piece, inserted one on an actor, and restarted the presses."

"Did you fire Gloria Parsons?"

"Yes, just as you instructed. She's down the hall, cleaning out her desk. Can you please tell me what this is all about?"

Charley Fox reached across the table and pulled the phone toward him. "Ms. Schwartz, this is Charles Fox, CEO of Triangle Partnership. Does that ring a bell?"

A moment's silence, then, "Yes, your company owns the magazine, doesn't it?"

"You're very quick, Ms. Schwartz. Now, I want you and Mr. Finch to listen to me very carefully. We are going to remake the magazine, or rather, you are, and before the next issue comes out. I want a completely new graphics look, modern and tasteful, and I want every piece written in that vein. We're going after a new audience."

"What sort of audience?" Hazel asked.

"Think *Town & Country.*"

Al Finch winced.

"I understand, Mr. Ford."

"Ms. Schwartz," Charley said, "if you don't think you can handle this, you can resign right now."

"I can handle it, Mr. Fox. Please leave it in my hands."

"I want to see the new design work daily, as it proceeds. E-mail it to me." He gave her the address.

"Yes, sir."

"Mr. Finch will be joining you to help out."

"Yes, sir, very good."

Charley broke the connection. "All right, Al, you can finish your soup now."

"Mr. Fox, I'm so sorry about all this. I had no idea . . ."

180

"Of course you didn't, Al. Now eat your soup, and when you're finished, grab a cab downtown and supervise the remake of *Just Folks.*"

"Yes, sir." Finch began to eat his soup, which was now cold. The waitress brought them lobster salad.

"Al," Charley said, "I want you to start featuring houses, apartments, and gardens in the magazine, those of well-known people in the arts, business, and professions."

"Mr. Fox," Al said, picking at his lobster, "I'm not sure how we're going to attract such people — at least, at first. We're not known for that sort of thing."

"Al, are you acquainted with Faith Mackey?"

"No, but I certainly know who she is."

"Well, *Just Folks* is her newest client. She's going to round up the people featured in the magazine and secure their cooperation."

"Well, that's wonderful," Finch said.

"I thought you'd think so," Charley replied, then he turned to his own lobster.

Fifteen minutes later, Al Finch was in a cab, headed downtown.

# 29

Gloria Parsons slammed her apartment door and flung the box containing the contents of her desk, mostly cosmetics, across the room, scattering them. The phone was ringing, but she was too angry to answer it. Finally, her answering machine picked up.

"Gloria, it's Hazel. I know you're angry, but we can do something about this. Call me as soon as you can. If Al Finch is in my office, I'll say I can't talk and call you back as soon as I can."

Gloria sat down and took some deep breaths, then called Hazel.

"This is Hazel."

"It's Gloria. What's going on?"

"I'm glad you called. First of all, the magazine is owned by a company called Triangle Partnership, which bought it from Christian St. Clair's estate. One of the triangle of partners is Stone Barrington."

Hazel waited for the explosion.

"Holy shit! Why didn't we know that?"

"I don't think even Barrington knew it. Certainly, I didn't. It's a good thing somebody caught it before it hit the newsstands."

"You said you know how to fix this."

"Not exactly fix it, just how to keep you employed."

"How?"

"First of all, one Charles Fox, the CEO of Triangle, has ordered that we completely redesign the magazine and its contents before the next issue. Al is on the way down here to work on it with me. Fox wants to go after the kind of audience that *Town & Country* attracts — upscale, older, et cetera, et cetera. Our new publicist is Faith Mackey. Got it?"

"Yeah, I guess. What does it have to do with me?"

"I want you to go on writing for the magazine, but under a new name. I've chosen one for you — Laurentia Scott-Peebles, known to her friends as Scotty. She's English, of a certain age — think tweed skirts and sensible shoes — writes well, of course. You'll have to invent a voice for her that matches that description. You won't be on staff — at least, not for a while — but I'll pay you top-dollar freelance rates.

You'll do a piece a month, and you have to find your first subject and get me a draft in forty-eight hours."

"What kind of piece?"

"Interiors, apartments, vacation homes, and gardens of people prominent in the arts, business, and the professions, with photographs. When you've picked a subject for your first piece, hire whatever photographer you want, and get it done."

"I've got an idea for the first piece."

"Who?"

"Let me get her signed on, then I'll tell you."

"Tell me now, so I can tell Al — it will show him I'm on board with the redesign."

"All right, the photographer Jamee Fellows. She's a sort of friend, and we can use her own photographs."

"A brilliant idea, Gloria! Excuse me — Scotty. I will address you that way from here on until . . ."

"Until what?"

"Until Stone Barrington dies or becomes senile, whichever happens first."

"He may die first," Gloria said. "I'll call you when I've spoken to Jamee." She hung up. "At least I won't starve," she said aloud to herself. She looked up Jamee Fellows's number and called her.

184

"Yeah?"

"Jamee, it's Gloria Parsons."

"Make it fast, kid, I'm working."

"We're completely redoing *Just Folks* as a very upmarket style publication, very posh indeed, and I want you to be my first subject — a glowing piece on your home and studio, using your own photographs. It will get great publicity — Faith Mackey is handling that."

"I'm impressed," Jamee said. "Okay, what do you need?"

"I need to record an interview with you to get some quotes and descriptions. First, e-mail me some photos that I can ask about."

"Okay."

"One other thing — I'm working under the name of Laurentia Scott-Peebles, an English writer. Call me Scotty."

"Explain that to me when I have more time."

"Okay, let's get rolling."

Jamee hung up.

Gloria called Hazel. "Okay, Jamee is on, she's sending me photos, then I'll interview her and write the piece."

As Hazel hung up, Al Finch walked into the office. "Okay, let's get started," he said.

"I've already got our art director redesigning the magazine. We'll have the first proofs this afternoon, and I've assigned the first cover story — it's the photographer Jamee Fellows."

"Wow," Al said. "That's fast work, kid. Who's writing it?"

"A woman named Laurentia Scott-Peebles, everybody calls her Scotty. We'll be using Jamee's own photographs. I'll have a first draft and pictures the day after tomorrow."

"I want to meet her," Al said.

"Not possible — she's reclusive, nobody even knows where she lives. She'll do the interviewing on the phone."

"Who the hell is she?"

"A very fine writer who's been teaching at Harvard and Oxford most of her life. I met her crossing on the *Queen Mary 2* last year, and we got on. I couldn't use her until now, she would never have worked for the old magazine."

"I can't wait to see her piece," Al said.

A young man knocked on Hazel's door.

"Hello, Art," Hazel said. "Al, this is Art, our art director. Al Finch, our publisher."

"That name will be easy to remember," Al said.

"I've got some proofs for you," Art said,

spreading the printouts on her desk.

"I like these," Hazel said.

"So do I," Al echoed. "I particularly like the title typeface. Approved."

"Go, Art," Hazel said, and he took his proofs and vanished.

"That was easy," Al said.

"Art is the best."

"Okay, let's talk about the rest of the magazine."

Hazel picked up some notes. "All right, we'll have a monthly feature on a gallery, along with the pictures they have in stock. They'll be lining up to get in. I want to hire a wine columnist and a food columnist. We'll do a sports feature, ones our readers play — tennis, golf, shooting, riding, et cetera. I know a woman who will be very good to edit and write those pieces."

"Hire her quick."

"Will do. We'll also do a series on giving dinner parties, everything from recipes to place settings, wines, and background music."

"Good," Al said. "I've got Faith Mackey coming here in an hour. I expect she'll have some ideas, too. She wants us to do a big party at a top restaurant to introduce the new magazine. We'll say we've been working on the redesign for months."

"I like that," Hazel said. Al went to take over the conference room, and Hazel put her head on her desk and wept with relief. She had saved her job.

# 30

Danny Blaine got the job at *W,* and he was thrilled. The pay was enough, the people were nice, and he got to choose who he slept with. He took Gloria Parsons to lunch on his first payday, and partially repaid her loan.

"You look happy," she said, as they sat down.

"What's not to be happy about?" he said. "I'm a free man, and there's not even a parole officer to check in with. I still can't believe it."

"You know what the first thing is you don't do?" she asked.

"What's that?"

"You don't go back to prison. Choose your friends better."

"I'm on board with that," he replied. They both ordered pasta. "You don't look quite as happy as I do," he said, scrutinizing her face. "What's up?"

"Well, I lost my job . . ." She held up a hand. "Not to worry, I got another one that may end up paying even better. I have to write under another name, though."

"What other name?"

"Laurentia Scott-Peebles."

"Sounds teddibly British."

"It is," she replied. "You can call me Scotty."

She explained the debacle of the Stone Barrington piece, and the consequences.

"You mean you were working for him the whole time and didn't know it?"

"*He* didn't know it. He's a partner in an investment firm, and the firm bought a bunch of companies, and one of them was *Just Folks.*"

"So he fired you."

"One of his partners did, and he changed the whole magazine, too. Now it's upscale and stylish, instead of tabloid semi-trash."

"Isn't that better?"

"It is if I freelance enough for them. Right now, I'm doing personality pieces, and garden and home stuff. I'm also a medium-rent dinner party advisor, under the name of Penelope Fairleigh, like the hotel uptown. I'm making almost as much as I did after my raise. If I knew anything about horses or shotguns, I'd be making even more."

"I don't like what this Barrington guy did to you."

"Well, neither do I, but I'm not stupid enough to try to do anything about it."

"I'm stupid enough," he said.

"No, baby, don't get involved."

"I don't mind being involved, if nobody knows it."

"He's bigger than you, sweetie."

"I'm not going to slug it out with him, I'm sneakier than that. What's his weak spot?"

"Sex. It's also his strong point."

"You sound regretful."

"Well, I didn't play it as well as I should have. Al Teppi looked into him and said he's the kind of guy I should marry and divorce, not somebody to dump."

"You dumped him?"

"I embarrassed him in print, which is worse, then he dumped me."

"No chance of putting it back together?"

She shook her head. "He won't even speak to me. I saw him at a big wedding reception, and he had me thrown out."

"That was a shitty thing to do."

"I know. I had to pay somebody two hundred bucks for the details so I could write my piece."

"Tell you what, let's both think about a

way to get even with him — and not get caught doing it."

"That's a nice thought," she said. They clinked their wineglasses and drank to it.

Stone got back from lunch with a friend, and Joan handed him a large envelope. "This just came from Charley Fox," she said.

Stone sat down at his desk and shook out the contents. The new *Just Folks* stared back at him, and he began leafing through it.

Joan buzzed. "Charley Fox on one."

Stone picked up the phone. "Hey, Charley, thanks for the new *Just Folks.*"

"Not bad, huh? I watched over its rebirth. I wasn't sure Al Finch and that editor, Hazel, had it in them."

"I like this piece on Jamee Fellows," Stone said. "I've always liked her work."

"That's by their new star writer, an Englishwoman named Laurentia Scott-Peebles."

"Never heard of her."

"She's a retired professor at Oxford, lives reclusively out on Long Island, and, I hear, she's in her sixties — too old for you."

"Oh, well."

"Listen, I should warn you — the new look for the magazine is going to cost us some circulation. Al Finch reckons we'll lose a million and a half before we come back."

"I hope he has a decent sales force to push the new look."

"That, and with Faith Mackey's help, he's throwing a big press party next week, to make a splash and get some attention. Faith is beating the bushes to get us some ink, too."

"Faith knows how to do that."

"There's an invitation in the mail. Will we see you there?"

"I'll be there. See you then." Stone nearly hung up, then remembered something. "Oh, Charley, I almost forgot. I'm going to need the yacht between Christmas and New Year's. That okay with you?"

"That's fine. That week Kaley and I are going skiing with Mike Freeman and his current."

"Perfect, then I won't have to clear it with him."

"Where are you going to be cruising? Surely not in Maine that time of the year."

"No, I'm headed for sunnier climes, but where is a secret."

"Why?"

"Some of my guests don't want to be noticed."

"That sounds mysterious."

"I'll tell you about it when it's over, and don't start questioning the captain. He and the crew are sworn to secrecy."

"I'm guessing a movie star. Or two."

"You can guess, but I will neither confirm nor deny."

"At least you can tell me where."

"No, I can't. When I'm finally able to explain, you'll understand perfectly why I couldn't."

"The islands?"

"Maybe, but I'm not telling you which islands."

"And there are too many to guess."

"There you go, pal. I hope it doesn't keep you up nights." Stone said goodbye and hung up.

# 31

Stone and Dino met at their club in the East Sixties, one so anonymous that it didn't have a name; the members called it, simply, "The Club." Dino called it "The Joint."

They met in the bar and had barely ordered a drink when Senator Eliot Saltonstall turned up, alone, and joined them.

"You throw a very nice bash, Eliot," Dino told him. "I've never had so much fun in a place that elegant."

"I may have to mortgage my house to pay the bill," the senator replied ruefully.

"I'm very impressed with your new son-in-law, Eliot," Stone said, "and so is my group at Woodman & Weld."

"It's nice to have a son-in-law I don't have to support," Saltonstall replied. "I had that problem with Celeste's older sister's first husband. I don't think I've ever been so relieved as when she divorced him."

"You think Peter can nail down the Senate seat in two years?" Stone asked.

"I think so, though I've heard a troubling rumor that Benton Blake is thinking seriously about running. He's already got a fully constructed political team, so Peter is going to have to run fast just to keep up."

"I'm good for a donation when he's ready," Stone said.

"Funny you should mention that," the senator said with a little smile. "You remember how Kate raised the money to get her campaign off the ground?"

"I remember." Stone had been one of a group of men who had donated a million dollars each to a political action committee formed for her benefit.

"Can I put you down for a million?"

"Of course," Stone said, hoping he didn't sound too regretful about it.

"Eliot," Dino said, "you can put me down for a round of applause when he gets elected. Stone and I float in different ponds."

"I couldn't ask a public servant for that kind of help, Dino, but I'll think of something else you can do."

"Uh-oh," Dino said, and they all laughed.

"I hear you two, along with Peter and Celeste, have a cruise planned shortly after Christmas."

"Don't breathe a word of that to anybody, Eliot," Stone said. "Our other guests don't want it to get out."

"I wonder why," the senator said. "Everybody's entitled to some time off. What's going on there?"

"I haven't asked, and I'm not going to," Stone replied.

"So be it. I'll keep my mouth shut."

"I'd appreciate that."

They finished their drinks and went in to dinner together.

Over the main course, Saltonstall looked around, then leaned in. "Dino," he said, "I wonder if there might be something in Benton Blake's background that he might not want mentioned to the voting public?"

"I'm not aware of anything, Eliot. I should think that having run twice for governor, anything like that would have emerged a long time ago."

"I'd be grateful for a heads-up if you should ever hear of anything," the senator said.

Dino shrugged noncommittally, but said nothing.

Saltonstall excused himself before dessert. "My wife's playing bridge, and she'll be home soon."

When he had gone, Dino lowered his

voice and said, "Can you believe that kind of question from a guy like Saltonstall?"

"He's a politician, Dino, and that's what his new son-in-law is going to be. He's just taking the long view."

"You mean he thinks the kid has a shot at something beyond the Senate?"

"Don't you think so?" Stone asked.

"Yeah, I guess I do," Dino replied.

Downtown, the governor of New York had swept the Chinese food off the table and was fucking the brains out of Gloria Parsons, who was doing everything she could think of to help. Only when they had come noisily did they repair to her bedroom, just for the rest.

"Is this getting to be a weekly date?" Gloria asked, her head on his hairy chest.

"Looks that way, doesn't it?" Blake replied.

"I can live with that," she said.

"How's your friend the ex-con doing?" he asked, changing the subject deftly.

"Very well, thanks to you. He's got a decent job at *W,* and he seems very happy."

"Glad to hear it," Blake replied. "Doing his part to keep the recidivism rate down, then?"

"You could say that."

"I hate it when somebody I've helped goes back — makes me look like I have poor judgment."

"I don't think you have to worry about him," Gloria said, toying with his genitalia. "Feeling like a little recidivism?"

"More and more," he said, pulling her on top of him. "Your turn to do all the work."

# 32

Stone was at his desk when Joan buzzed him. "Bob Cantor is here," she said.

"Send him in."

Bob walked into the office, they shook hands, then he sat down.

The other Bob, the Labrador retriever, wandered into the office, sniffed at Cantor, approved, and lay down with his head on the man's foot.

"Bob, have you met Bob?"

"He's named for me?"

"No, it's just a coincidence. His mother whelped a large litter, and she was running out of names."

"I see. Would you like a report?"

"Shoot."

"I followed Gloria Parsons from her office to Alphonse Teppi's loft, where the two had a conversation about you." He placed a recording device on Stone's desk and pressed a button.

Stone listened carefully. "Ah, that's where the piece about my murdering my wife came from."

"Did she try that?"

"She did, and she got fired for her trouble."

"I heard something about that during my surveillance," Bob said. "She's back at work, though."

"At *Just Folks*?"

"Under a new name, Laurentia Scott-Peebles, known as Scotty. She's also writing a dinner party column under the name of Penelope Fairleigh. She's making slightly more as a freelancer than she made on staff."

"I don't seem to be able to get rid of her."

"You want me to do something about it?"

"No, just let it ride. She's a good writer, I'll give her that, even under the two pseudonyms. I'll just keep the knowledge as ammunition for a later date."

"She also managed to get Danny Blaine out of Fishkill."

"How the hell did she do that?"

"By fucking the governor. Blake commuted the kid's sentence."

"Well now, that's interesting on two counts," Stone said.

"It's apparently getting to be a weekly

thing," Bob said. "They talked about it in bed."

"I know someone who needs to know this," Stone said, "but not until the proper time. Have you made tapes?"

"Yes."

"Please continue to do so."

"She also had lunch with Danny and told him about being fired from the magazine. He wants revenge, but she's told him to cool it, she doesn't want him to go back to prison, and by the way, neither does the governor."

"Well, that shows restraint. Stay on her, and let's see what else turns up."

"As you wish. I gave Joan my bill to date."

"Thanks, Bob, and keep those reports coming in."

The two men shook hands, and Bob left. The other Bob didn't even notice the removal of his pillow; he just snored on.

Joan buzzed him. "Peter Rule on one."

"Peter? How are you?"

"Very well, Stone. Are you, by chance, free for lunch today?"

"Yes, I am."

"I saw your name on the Yacht Club's newly elected members' list this morning. Why don't we meet there? Twelve-thirty?"

"See you then."

Stone had nearly forgotten that he had been proposed for membership. Those wheels ground slowly, he guessed. He had gone most of his life without joining any kind of club, and now he belonged to three, and he didn't mind a bit.

They met in the bar, then moved into the beautiful dining room, which had been designed at the turn of the last century to resemble the belowdecks of a ship, and ordered seafood, which seemed appropriate.

"Celeste and I are looking forward to our cruise," Peter said, "and I know Mom appreciates your keeping it quiet. She has something in mind, but I don't know what it is."

"We'll just wait for the surprise, then."

"The senator tells me you're pitching in on his new PAC. I'm very grateful to you, Stone."

"I'm glad to help. I think it's a good idea for a wealthy politician not to contribute too visibly to his own campaign, and it's just as important to adhere to the letter of the campaign laws."

"I fully intend to do that."

"When do you expect to announce?"

"Perhaps a year before the election, depending on circumstances."

"Depending on whether Benton Blake throws in?"

"Ah, the senator told you about the rumor?"

"Yes, and he could be a formidable competitor. After all, the people have already elected him to statewide office twice."

"I think the divorce is hurting him," Peter said. "He's loath to give his wife half his money and a house, but if he stiffs her, it will hurt him at election time."

"Not a good position to be in," Stone agreed. "Peter, I'm impressed with your clean record, but there's something else you should consider."

"What's that?"

"What happened in London."

Peter looked confused. "Did something happen in London?"

"That will be the question on the minds of the operatives who handle Benton's or your other opponents' campaigns. You might reflect on those years, as well as those at Princeton and Harvard, and dredge up anything that might be termed misbehavior, especially with regard to women. It would be much easier to deal with such matters now, rather than later."

"You have a point."

"For instance, are there any little Peters running around in New Jersey or Cambridge?"

"No, nothing like that. I tend to be a serial monogamist where the ladies are concerned, so there were only a relative few."

"How about at Oxford, when you were studying there?"

"Ah, I loved English girls."

"Very many?"

"More than at school in the States. There's an old joke about what women of different nationalities say immediately after having made love."

"Tell me."

"A German girl says, '*Gut,* now let's have somesing to eat!' A French girl says, 'You weel improve wiz practice.' An American girl says, 'Now you must think I'm awful.' But an English girl says, 'There, dear, is that better?' I like that attitude."

Stone laughed. "You'll remember that Jack Kennedy's older brother, Joe Junior, was killed in an accident during World War Two, when an airplane he was flying that was filled with explosives went off before he could depart the aircraft."

"Yes, I knew that."

"One account of that time in his life says

he was living with an Englishwoman near his base who had a couple of children and a husband overseas."

"That, I didn't know."

"It's the sort of thing that, especially in those days, would have come back to haunt him if he had lived to run for President."

"I see your point, Stone. Don't worry, the skeletons in my closet are things like the time I got drunk at a Harvard party and threw up on a dean's shoes."

Stone laughed. "Well, we all have stories like that."

"I appreciate your concern, Stone, and I'll be very careful."

"Please tell Celeste she needs to be careful, too, and ask her to review her past associations for any sign of trouble."

"I'll broach the subject."

# 33

Peter Rule had a couple of afternoon meetings with local politicos, then got home around six, to find Celeste hanging pictures in their living room. They kissed.

"Nice," he said, checking out the art. "Where did these come from?"

"I found them in Dad's attic," she said, "just gathering dust. I thought we could make better use of them."

"I like them," he said. "Can I buy you a drink?"

"Oh, yes, thank you. I'll get us a snack." She went into the kitchen and came back with some pâté and crackers.

He handed her her usual scotch, and they settled into the living room sofa. "I had lunch with Stone Barrington today," he said.

"Oh? Why?"

"I was at the Yacht Club and had some time on my hands, so I called him and he came over. Your dad told me that Stone is going to give a million bucks to the new PAC, and I wanted to thank him."

"Wow! That's generous of him."

"It's more than he'll get from fees on our legal work," Peter said. "He gave me some good advice, too."

"What sort of advice?"

"Your dad told him about a rumor that Benton Blake is going to run for the Senate seat."

"*Your* Senate seat?"

Peter laughed. "Best not to refer to it that way until I'm actually elected to it."

"I suppose."

"Stone suggested that I dredge my memories of Princeton, Harvard, Oxford, and London for anything that Benton or any other opponent might use against me during the campaign."

"I can't wait to hear what you came up with," she said.

"I'm afraid the worst I could do was when I got drunk at Harvard and threw up on a dean's shoes."

"Pretty tough to get an attack ad out of that, isn't it?"

"I think what he really wanted to know was if I had any little Rules running around in any of those places."

"And do you?"

"Certainly not! What's the Pill for, after all?"

She didn't laugh.

"He also suggested that you take a trip down memory lane and see if there's anything there that might raise a voter's eyebrow."

"Well, I'll have to rewind that tape and see what I can come up with," she said.

He noted that she still wasn't laughing, which was unlike her.

"Okay . . . find anything on the tape?"

"You mean I get all of half a minute to reflect?"

"I didn't mean to rush you. Were there all that many men in your past?"

"A few," she said, looking pensive.

"Anyone or anything I should know about?"

"Maybe," she said.

Peter took her glass, went to the bar, and made them another drink, then came back and sat down. She was distractedly looking out the window over the park.

He handed her the drink and thought it best not to press things.

"There was something," she said. "I didn't think I would ever tell anyone about it, but if I can't tell you, then what sort of marriage would we have?"

"I don't mean to pry," Peter said, "and neither did Stone. I think he's right for us to think about these things, and if there's anything, then deal with it now instead of during a campaign."

"He has a point."

Peter set down his drink, took her face in his hands, and kissed her. "I'm sorry I brought it up. Let's just forget about it."

"No," she said, "Stone is right — now is better than later." She took a swig of her drink and took a deep breath. "I had something of a fling on the Vineyard, the summer after my freshman year at Mount Holyoke. With an older man who was renting the house next to ours for the summer."

"Well, I've had a few flings in my time — you're entitled."

"But he was married."

"Oh."

"A friend of Dad's."

"Oh."

"And I got pregnant."

"Oooooh. How did you handle that?"

"He researched it and gave me the name of a clinic on the mainland. I took the ferry over one day and had an abortion. It went well. I paid cash — he had given me the money — and I was home in time for a nap before dinner."

"That was it?"

"That was it. I never saw him again. I mean, I saw him around, but I was never alone with him again. It only happened twice."

"Who else knew about it at the time?"

"Nobody."

"You didn't tell a girlfriend, or anybody else?"

"No, I was too ashamed."

"Nothing to be ashamed about. You made a mistake, that's all."

They were both quiet for a minute.

"Sweetheart," he said, "is there any reason to worry about us having children?"

"Oh, no," she said. "I mean, I don't have any reason to think that. The doctor at the clinic said that it all went very well, and there was no reason to worry about any health consequences."

"Did you use your own name at the clinic?"

"Of course not! I was young but I wasn't stupid." She sighed. "Well, I suppose it was stupid to get involved with him in the first place."

"You were young, as you say. Do you think you have any lingering psychological issues?"

"No, I tried to put it behind me, and by

the time I got back to school, I think I pretty much had. Honestly, I think that he was more upset than I. I mean, he had a wife and a child and a career ahead. I suppose he wondered if I could keep a secret, but he didn't really have to worry about that — I didn't want anyone to know, and no one ever did, until now."

"I'm glad that you could tell me. It makes me love you all the more."

She kissed him. "You're sweet, and I love you, too."

They put down their drinks, and in a moment they were undressed and making love on the sofa.

They lay in each other's arms and slept for a few minutes, then she stirred. "Peter," she said.

He turned over and raised himself on an elbow.

"Yes?"

"There is one other person who knows."

"Who?"

"*He* knows."

"Well, there is that."

"I don't think he would want it known now, in the circumstances."

"What circumstances?"

"The campaign."

"Are you concerned about blackmail? Would he do that?"

"Of course not, after all, he has a stake in this, too."

"Do I need to know who he is?"

"I think you do."

"Then tell me."

"It was Benton Blake."

# 34

Benton Blake stabbed a chunk of sweet-and-sour chicken and chewed thoughtfully. "I made a decision today," he said.

Gloria set down her chopsticks, sensing a significant moment. "Tell me," she said, preparing for the worst.

"I'm definitely not running again. In fact, I may resign before my term is up next year."

"Congratulations," she said, relieved that he didn't seem to be dumping her.

"We're finally getting somewhere on the divorce settlement," he said. "I think we'll wrap it up soon, and I'll be a free man."

"Congratulations again," she said. "Why would you want to resign before your term is up?"

"I'm going to have to give Vanessa pretty much half of everything, and I'm going to want to make some money before I have to start campaigning."

"What do you want to do?"

"Well, I'm an attorney, you know. I was very successful before I became governor, and I can be even more so again. Any law firm would be pleased to have a former governor as a partner — his contacts in state government could be invaluable."

"I can understand that."

"Also, I don't want to wait another year before I can be seen in public with you. I feel guilty that all we can have is Chinese food and great sex."

"Correction," she said, "fabulous sex."

"No argument there, but I want to be able to take you out to dinner and to the theater and to dinner parties. That would be worth what I'd have to give up for an early settlement."

"I'm flattered that you think so." She really was; she was beginning to think this thing between them might have a future.

"I'm going to put out a feeler to a firm tomorrow. I have friends there, and I know they'll keep my confidence."

"Benton, do you think Vanessa has been seeing anybody?"

"Oh, I'm sure of it," he replied. "She always manages to be in New York when I'm in Albany, or in the Hamptons when I'm in New York. We rarely see each other anymore."

"Do you know who he is?"

"No. I've racked my brain, and I don't think it can be anybody I know."

"If you could find out, you might be able to sue on grounds of adultery and achieve a better settlement."

"You'd make a pretty good lawyer, you know?"

"Thank you."

"No, that would be a protracted thing, with a public trial. It would be a mess, and it would put you in jeopardy."

"In jeopardy for what?" she asked.

"Well, if I should put a private detective on her and she found out, she could put one on me, and you might be exposed."

"I suppose that could happen," she said. She was grateful to him for wanting to protect her.

She took their dishes into the kitchen and put the leftovers into the fridge. He came and stood behind her, holding her close, and she could tell he was more than ready.

He turned her around, picked her up, and set her on the kitchen counter, then pulled off her thong. She raised herself enough for him to push her dress above her waist, and he was at exactly the right height to enter her, no lubricant required.

■ ■ ■ ■

They showered together afterward, then got into bed and did it again and lay, panting, in each other's arms.

"This is what I want," he said. "Is this what you want?"

"Yes," she said without hesitation. They were only a few weeks into this relationship, but she knew this was what she wanted.

"I'll need a couple of weeks to get the settlement signed, then I'll resign, and everyone will think it's because I'm depressed over the divorce. A few weeks after that, you and I can be seen in public, and we'll be married before I announce for the Senate."

"Married?" she asked, sitting up.

"Is that not what you want?"

"I want it, I just didn't think it was possible."

"I'm an impatient man," he said, pulling her down to him again.

"Will my being in your life be a negative thing for the campaign?"

"No, we're a good fourteen, fifteen months away from announcing, I think."

"I wouldn't want for anyone to use me against you."

"Listen, I'm squeaky clean. The press has gotten used to that, and they won't blame me for starting to see someone else after that."

"Squeaky clean?" she laughed.

"There's only one thing in my past that I would worry about."

She didn't ask; she wanted it to come from him.

"Some years ago I had a summer fling on the Vineyard with the daughter of a friend, my next-door neighbor. She was a college girl at the time. It only happened a couple of times, but she got pregnant."

"Is she likely to be a problem?"

"No, it's not like that. She got an abortion, and we didn't see each other again, except socially. Anyway, in the circumstances, she would have as much to lose as I if it came up during a campaign."

Stone was working when Bob Cantor turned up and took a seat in his office.

"There have been developments," he said.

"Tell me."

"Gloria Parsons has got her hooks into Benton Blake."

"Well, we've known about that for weeks."

"No, this is all new." He set the little recorder on Stone's desk and played the conversation. "This just happened last night, and I got it off the autorecorder this morning."

Stone listened to the whole tape. "Well," he said, "looks like Benton is serious about this affair. I don't know whether I underestimated or overestimated him."

"She's quite the looker," Bob said, "and it sounds as if he's really going all in."

"I don't suppose you have any idea who his wife is screwing," Stone said.

"You haven't asked me to look into that, but I will if that's what you want."

"No, I'm not really interested in his marriage, I just wanted something on Gloria, in case I needed it."

"Well, you have that."

"And now that I do, I don't want it," Stone said. "In fact, I feel guilty about having initiated this — it's none of my business, really."

"I can understand why you might feel that way," Bob said. "Do you want me to terminate the investigation?"

"I don't care about what goes on in her apartment or her love life, but I do care about any conversations she might have with Danny Blaine or Alphonse Teppi that concern me."

"Okay, I'll stay on it, then." They shook

hands, and Bob left.

Joan came into his office and handed him a note. "Bill Eggers's secretary called while you were meeting with Bob. She wants to know if you're available for lunch tomorrow with Bill at The Club at one o'clock."

"Tell her I'm available," Stone said.

# 35

Stone arrived at The Club a little early and found Bill Eggers ahead of him in the bar. They ordered drinks.

"I'm glad we have a moment to talk before Benton gets here," Eggers said.

"What's it about?"

"I've heard that he's interested in practicing law again, when his term is up."

Stone tried to look surprised. "Do you think he could make some rain?"

"I think he could produce a few thunderstorms. Remember, he appointed all the heads of the state agencies — now he can reap the benefits, and there's nothing unethical about it."

"Would you bring him in as a partner?"

"Absolutely, that's where he'd be the most effective."

"I agree," Stone said.

"And there's something else. Benton has hinted strongly that he's going to run for the Senate at the midterm, so he wouldn't be around for much more than a year. By that time we'd have reaped about all from the state that we're going to."

"Could he be senator and a partner simultaneously?"

"He wouldn't be the first," Eggers said, "but in those circumstances we wouldn't be paying him as much."

"Suppose he loses the Senate race?"

"To whom?"

"Well, I expect someone could crop up, perhaps even someone who could beat him."

"In that case, he could continue with the firm, but his compensation would be based on the business he brings in, so that's okay with me."

"It's okay with me, too," Stone said.

Eggers was about to say something else, but Benton Blake appeared in the bar, and they sat down for lunch.

"Long time," Blake said to Stone.

"I don't get to Albany much," Stone replied, "and I didn't see you at the Saltonstall wedding dinner."

"I had to be in California to entice a tech company to relocate in upstate New York."

"Successful?"

"I believe so. We'll know after their next

board meeting, which is in a couple of weeks."

"Good luck."

"And I want to thank both of you for your support over the past two terms. It's meant a lot to me, more than just the money."

"You're very welcome, Benton," Eggers said. "Tell me, have you given any thought to what you're going to do when your time as governor is done?"

That's making it easy for him, Stone thought.

"I have, Bill. I want to practice law again."

"That's very interesting, Benton. When you get closer to the end of your term, let's talk seriously about that. I'm sure we could find a nice office for you at Woodman & Weld."

"I'm nearer to the end of my term than you know, Bill, so let's talk about it now."

"Tell me what I don't know."

"We're wrapping up my divorce agreement now, and as soon as that's completed, I plan to resign as governor."

"What's the rush?" Eggers asked.

"I'm considering a run for the Senate in two years, and I want to do some good for myself before I do."

"Well, Benton, we'd be delighted to have you at Woodman & Weld as a partner."

"I'm delighted to hear that, and I'm sure we can work out something."

"I'm sure about that, too." Eggers extended a hand. "Welcome aboard, Benton."

Stone shook his hand, too. "How long before you can join us, Benton?"

"Within a month. I'm going over to my lawyer's office after lunch to read the final agreement. If it's satisfactory, I'll sign it and as soon as the court accepts it and issues a decree, I'll resign."

"I'll go back to the office and dictate an offer," Eggers said, "and e-mail it to you. You'll have it to read by the end of the day, and we can hash out the details soon. We'll be ready to welcome you as soon as you leave Albany."

Eggers ordered a bottle of champagne, and they toasted the new relationship.

Stone rode with Eggers back to the Seagram Building, where the offices of Woodman & Weld were located. He wanted to drop in on his group and see how they were doing. "Bill, can I tell my people about this?"

"Wait until Benton has signed on the dotted line. Anyway, nothing he does will affect what goes on in your group."

"All right," Stone said. They got out of

the car in the garage and took the elevator to the top floor, where both their offices were located. Stone thanked Eggers for lunch and went to the suite of offices occupied by The Barrington Group. Herbie Fisher was on his computer amid the ruins of a brown bag lunch.

"How's it going, Stone?"

"Very well, thanks, Herb. Is everything running smoothly here?" He took a seat on the sofa.

"We're shipshape," Herbie said. "I'm glad to see you. I was going to call this afternoon anyway."

"What's up?"

"I heard a rumor from a reliable source that Benton Blake is going to resign and go back to practicing law."

"Who is this reliable source?" Stone asked, surprised.

"Vanessa Blake," he said.

"How the hell do you know Vanessa Blake?" Stone asked.

"My house in the Hamptons is a couple of doors down the beach from theirs. We both run every morning, and that's how we bumped into each other."

"Anything going on there, Herb?"

"No. Not that I wouldn't enjoy that, but she's already got a boyfriend. Anyway, that's how I heard about Benton's plans," he said. "During one of our conversations, Vanessa told me he wants to practice law again. You and Eggers should make him an offer — he'd be a great rainmaker."

"What a good idea," Stone said. "I'll mention it to Bill."

# 36

Stone and Dino met for dinner at Patroon.

"You look pretty happy," Dino said. "What's been going on?"

"You wouldn't believe it," Stone replied, causing some of his bourbon to vanish.

"Don't I always believe it?"

"Believe what?"

"Believe you."

"Well, yeah, after you've grilled me for a few minutes to see if there are any holes in my story. Any conversation with you is always an interrogation."

"That's a dirty communist lie," Dino replied. "I'm a charming conversationalist."

"Right up to, but not including, the rubber hose."

"The rubber hose went out with spats," Dino said. "These days we use a New York City telephone book — the black pages, not the yellow ones, or the Sunday *Times*. Both make more noise than the rubber hose and leave less bruising."

"Well, I'm glad to be brought up to date with the latest in police violence," Stone said. "Now, are you ready to converse normally?"

"Who did you have lunch with today at The Club?"

"There you go again, can't you just pretend to listen quietly and murmur an occasional encouraging noise?"

"Ah, um," Dino replied.

"Okay, here we go — Benton and Vanessa Blake are divorcing."

"Um, ah," Dino said, resting his chin on his hand, elbow on the table. "Been there, heard that."

"Benton is screwing Gloria Parsons."

"Aha! What else?"

"Let's see . . . Oh, yes, Benton is going to resign the governorship and come to Woodman & Weld as a partner, where he will, Bill Eggers hopes, make it rain all the time."

"Now *that's* news."

"He's also going to marry Gloria Parsons."

Dino shook his head. "Benton has been married for so long he's forgotten that these days you don't have to marry 'em to fuck 'em. Somebody should explain that to him before he does something crazy."

"And then Benton is going to run for the

Senate against Peter Rule, except he doesn't know yet that Peter is running."

"I'd like to see his face when he finds out. Now tell me some dirt."

"That's not enough dirt for you?" Stone asked.

Stone sighed and lowered his voice. "All right, but this is the kind of news I don't share with anybody, not even you, usually."

"I will take it to my grave," Dino said solemnly.

"If you tell anybody, even Viv, I'll see that that happens sooner rather than later."

Dino made the motion of locking his lips with a key.

"Before he was governor, Benton used to rent a house on the Vineyard, right next door to Eliot Saltonstall's house."

"Yeah? What's so hot about that?"

"He dallied with the girl next door."

"Eliot's daughter? Which one?"

"Celeste, the younger one."

"The one who's now married to Peter Rule?"

"The very one."

"And how did that turn out?"

"She found herself pregnant."

"Now *that's* dirt!" Dino said.

"And she had an abortion."

"All this with a girl who married the guy

who's running against Benton for the Senate?"

"That is correct."

"Stone, I've gotta hand it to you, when asked for dirt, you come up in spades. In fact, you should carry around a spade, just to handle it."

"I'm so glad to have entertained you," Stone said.

Then dinner came.

# 37

Stone was in his office the following morning when Joan buzzed. "Senator Saltonstall on one," she said.

Stone pressed the button. "Good morning, Eliot," he said.

"Good morning, Stone," the senator said. "Have you heard the rumors?"

"What rumors?" Stone asked cautiously.

"There are so many I can't keep track of them."

"Rumors about what?"

"Rumors about everybody and everything," the senator said. "I hear that the Benton Blakes are divorcing. I hear that they both have lovers. I hear that Benton is resigning the governorship."

"It sounds as if all that remains is for Benton to find himself pregnant."

*"What?"*

"Sorry, Eliot, that was an attempt at humor."

"Don't confuse me with humor, I'm confused enough as it is. Have you heard these rumors?"

"I have now," Stone replied.

"Have you heard that Benton is going to declare for the Senate?"

"I think that's a logical thing for him to do, considering all the rumors."

"Do you think he's planning to practice law again?"

"Well, he's a lawyer. We were at law school together, but a year apart."

"Do you think he might join Woodman & Weld?"

"If that's another rumor, the only person who could comment on it, besides Blake, is Bill Eggers."

"Have you heard any other rumors?"

"I don't get out much, Eliot. These things tend to pass me by."

"I'm still trying to find something on Benton, and it's more important than ever. Have you heard anything on that score?"

Stone paused. He could hardly tell the man that Blake had seduced his daughter, fathered a potential grandchild for him, then paid for the abortion. After all, the girl was Saltonstall's daughter and his candidate's wife. "Not a thing," he replied finally.

"Why your delay in answering?"

"I was scouring my brain for signs of a rumor but found none."

"If Blake runs for the Senate, do you think he could defeat Peter?"

Stone thought for a moment. "After scouring my brain again, I don't know. They both have big advantages as a candidate. I should think it would be close, maybe a toss-up."

"That's what I think, too," the senator said, "and it's why I'm trying so hard to find something on Blake."

"Just relax and don't try so hard, Eliot. If there's something out there, it will likely surface before Election Day. Anyway, you don't want people to know that you're trying to torpedo Benton before he's even announced. You could start a rumor."

"That's what I like about you, Stone, you give thoughtful, sensible advice, even if you're not much on rumors."

"Thank you, Eliot, I think."

"There's a rumor that you, Blake, and Bill Eggers had lunch yesterday at The Club."

"Bill and I had a lunch date, and we ran into Benton." That was very, very close to being the truth.

"So it wasn't a rumor?"

"I suppose not, in the circumstances."

"What circumstances?"

"That the three of us lunched together

yesterday."

"Oh, yes. Did you discuss the election?"

"We talked mostly about the law, as I recall." And where Blake was going to practice it, but he didn't mention that. "When is Peter contemplating an announcement?" Stone asked, hoping for a change of subject.

"Well, our first thought was about a year out from the election, but if Blake announces sometime soon, that could change."

"I suppose that, if they both announce, that might discourage other potential office-seekers."

"That's a very good point and an argument for an early announcement. Perhaps Peter should announce before Blake has a chance to."

"Do you think Peter's announcing would discourage Blake from doing so?"

"That's a very good question, Stone, and one I'll have to contemplate at length. Do you have an opinion?"

"Well, off the top of my head, I would think that Blake possesses sufficient ego to cause him to think of Peter as a kid and not much in the way of competition. It couldn't hurt to have Blake underestimate Peter and his chances."

"Hmmmm," Saltonstall responded.

"I hope I've been helpful," Stone said.

"You've certainly given me food for thought, Stone. Are you free for lunch today?"

Stone didn't want to prolong this conversation. "I'm afraid not, Eliot, and I have a client waiting to see me now, so I'd better run."

"Of course. Let me know if you hear any rumors."

"Take care, Eliot." He hung up and buzzed Joan.

"Yes, boss?"

"If Senator Saltonstall calls back before lunch, tell him I'm with a client."

"Gotcha."

Stone called Dino.

"Bacchetti."

"Have you heard any new rumors?"

"Why do you ask?"

"Because Eliot Saltonstall just called me and related most of what I told you last night."

"You think I blabbed to Saltonstall?"

"Of course not, Dino. I trust you implicitly. I just wonder where he's hearing this stuff."

"Apparently everybody is hearing it because I've heard most of it from at least two people this morning."

"How much of it?"

"Just about everything except the pregnancy thing."

"Did you hear Gloria Parsons's name mentioned?"

"Come to think of it, no. Do you want me to start that rumor?"

"Good God, no — we don't want Benton's name sullied before he can join Woodman & Weld."

"But after that, it's okay?"

"Not until we've milked him dry."

# 38

The following morning, Stone received another call from Senator Eliot Saltonstall.

"Good morning, Stone."

"Good morning, Eliot."

"With regard to our conversation of yesterday, and the possible forthcoming announcement that Benton Blake is declaring for the Senate, Peter and I have decided that he should announce first."

"And when will that be?" Stone asked.

"Preferably the day before Benton plans to announce."

"And what date will that be?"

"Frankly, Stone, I was hoping you could tell me. After all, you hear things."

"Eliot, when I hear things I, more than likely, hear them from you, as I did yesterday."

"All right, then how about the day before Benton announces his resignation from the governorship."

"Eliot, it may surprise you to learn that the governor does not report his intentions to me on any sort of regular basis. I think it would be more productive if you back-tracked."

"Backtracked? What does that mean?"

"It means that you should call the person or persons who passed on to you the rumors that you passed on to me yesterday and ask them for any further rumors."

"But why should those persons have information any better than what you could get?"

"That would seem obvious, if you think about it."

The senator paused for a moment. "All right, I've thought about it, and I think you are as good a source as they."

"Eliot, I don't know, nor have I heard any rumor concerning the date of Benton's announcement."

"But surely you know someone who knows."

"Not only do I not know anyone who knows, I have no idea whether Benton himself knows. I think he did say he would do so after his property settlement had been approved by the court."

"And when will that be?"

"I got the impression that it should be

sooner, rather than later."

"That's very imprecise, Stone."

"I'm aware of that, but it's all I know — or think I know. May I make a suggestion?"

"Of course."

"I expect that, over the course of your political life, you have come to know a person or persons who work for or have regular dealings with the family court."

"I expect so."

"Then perhaps you could call one or more of those persons and make inquiries. For instance, it might be helpful to know which judge is presiding over Blake v. Blake, would it not?"

"I expect it would."

"Perhaps you might even be socially acquainted with that judge, and if you took him to lunch or engaged him in conversation on the subject of the Blakes, he might refer to the status of their petition."

"Perhaps you could do that for me?"

"Eliot, since I have never handled a divorce as an attorney, nor have I been divorced, I have no knowledge of the inner workings or personnel of the family court."

"Oh."

"Yes."

"Yes, what?"

"I was responding to your 'oh.' "

"Oh."

"Yes."

"Let's not start this again," the senator said.

"No."

"Perhaps Bill Eggers might have a better idea than you of the timeline in question."

"Why do you think that, Eliot?"

"Well, if Benton is going to join Woodman & Weld upon his resignation as governor, that might relate to the date of his joining Woodman & Weld, and we could work from that time."

Stone sighed. "All right, Eliot, I'll ask Bill if Benton is going to join us, and if so, when. I think that's all I can do."

"That would be most helpful, Stone, and I would be most grateful."

"I'll get back to you." They said goodbye, and Stone called Eggers and was connected.

"Good morning, Bill."

"Good morning, Stone."

"Eliot Saltonstall is driving me crazy," Stone said.

"That could be the title of a popular song," Eggers said, "as in 'You, You're Driving Me Crazy.' "

"Perhaps in an earlier era," Stone replied.

"Why is he driving you crazy?"

"He wants to know the exact date Benton

Blake will resign as governor."

"Why?"

"So that Peter Rule can announce for the Senate before Benton has a chance to."

"Peter is running for the Senate?"

Stone slapped his forehead. "I seem to have inadvertently started a rumor to that effect. Is it too late to swear you to secrecy?"

"I'll be happy to keep your secret, Stone — or rather, Peter's secret."

"Thank you. I would not like to have Eliot trace such a rumor back to me."

"I understand entirely."

"Do you know the date Benton will resign?"

"I do."

"Would it entail a breach of confidence if you were to tell me that date?"

"It would."

"Oh."

"But I'll tell you anyway, just to give young Peter a leg up on his announcement."

"Thank you."

There was a long silence, which Stone finally broke.

"Bill?"

"Yes?"

"You were going to give me the date of Blake's announcement."

"Oh, yes, I'm sorry, my mind wandered

for a moment. The date. Now, let's see — Benton expects Judge Ellis to approve his property settlement next Friday, and if he does so, Blake will make his announcement early on the following Monday, so as to make the morning shows."

"Ah, thank you."

"Of course, if Judge Ellis gets busy or something, that could change."

"Of course. Thank you, Bill. I'll pass that on to Eliot." They hung up, and Stone called Saltonstall.

"Yes, Stone?"

"Here's what I've learned, Eliot. It is expected that Judge Ellis, who is presiding, will approve the Blakes' property settlement next Friday, and if so, Benton will announce his resignation early on the following Monday, so as to make the morning shows."

"That's wonderful news, Stone. Is that a certainty?"

"No, it's a target date, subject to change for all sorts of reasons, and you should treat it as no more than that."

"That's troubling."

"Life is troubling, Eliot."

"All right, then I'll suggest that Peter announce next Friday."

"I hope it all works out, Eliot."

"Oh, I expect it will. Goodbye, Stone."

"Goodbye, Eliot."
They both hung up. Stone was exhausted.

# 39

The following Friday, Stone was watching *Morning Joe* with his breakfast when Mika Brzezinski broke off an interview with some politico, pressed a finger to her ear, and said, "Hold on, we have breaking news. Let's go to the Capitol in Washington, D.C., where Senator Eliot Saltonstall is making a statement."

The scene switched to the steps of the Capitol; fortunately, the sun was shining brightly. Eliot Saltonstall stood at a bank of microphones with a couple of dozen people, some of them United States senators, gathered behind him. "Good morning," the senator said. "This is an important announcement for the people of New York State and of the United States. I wish to introduce to you Peter Rule, who, four years ago joined my Senate staff as a junior assistant and who has since risen quickly to be, first my senior legislative advisor and then, my chief of staff. The people of New York State have come to know him as a supremely competent Senate staffer who has dealt with our constituents from Buffalo to New York City, helping to solve their problems with their government. Peter has an announcement to make. Peter?" Saltonstall stood aside and left the microphones to the younger man.

"Good morning," Peter said, in a rich, deep voice. "Today I am privileged to announce my candidacy for the seat in the United States Senate being vacated at midterm by Senator Len Scott. I will work, hand in hand with Senator Eliot Saltonstall, who will become senior senator and who has given me the honor of representing his staff in every corner of the state, an experience that has deepened my knowledge of our citizens' problems and expectations of their government. Between now and the election I will put forward a detailed program for our state and the nation, but for now, I will let you return to your breakfast. Thank you."

The group behind him applauded and cheered, and Senator Saltonstall shook his hand.

The scene shifted back to *Morning Joe.* "That was the newest candidate for the

United States Senate, Peter Rule. For those of you not acquainted with him, here are his biographical details." She read from a sheet of paper:

"Peter Rule is the son of the late Simon Rule, a high official of the Central Intelligence Agency for many years, and the current President of the United States, Katharine Rule Lee, who was formerly director of Central Intelligence. He is a graduate of Princeton, with a bachelor's in constitutional history, and Harvard, where he earned a master's and a Ph.D. in American political history. He also studied at Oxford for a year as a Rhodes Scholar. After completing his education, Mr. Rule joined a London investment bank, where, while also attending the London School of Economics and earning another Ph.D., in economics, he specialized in international lending. He is currently chief of staff to Senator Eliot Saltonstall, of New York, and he was recently married to Senator Saltonstall's younger daughter, Celeste. They live in New York City and in Georgetown."

The discussion was thrown open to the group around *Morning Joe*'s table, who seemed all to be favorably impressed with the new candidate's credentials.

"I know this young man well," said John

Heilemann, a frequent contributor to the show, "and anyone crazy enough to run against him is going to have his hands full." Everyone at the table seemed to agree with him.

In Albany, the governor of New York State, Benton Blake, threw his breakfast tray across the room and screamed obscenities, alarming two members of his staff, who rushed into the room to clean up after him.

That night, Gloria Parsons cradled Benton in her arms. "Don't worry about it, baby," she cooed. "You'll take this kid with one hand tied behind your back."

Benton sat up in bed. "Listen," he said, "this kid is the son of the current President of the United States and the stepson of the former President of the United States, not to mention being the son-in-law of the other senator from New York and the husband of his daughter, possibly the most beautiful woman on the North American continent. From what I've learned, he knows this state better than anybody else alive, including me. That is what I'm up against, and I am going to need not only both my hands, but every brain cell in my possession and half the money in the state to defeat him. Now do you understand why I'm upset?"

"Well," said Gloria, "you don't *have* to run against him. You can run for another term as governor or just join Woodman & Weld and make a lot of money, then wait for Eliot Saltonstall to have a stroke or something, so you can run for *his* seat."

Benton fell back onto the bed. "I hate this," he said. "I just *hate* it."

She began fondling him. "It's going to be all right, baby," she cooed. "You're going to have the most *wonderful* life. And," she said, "you can take consolation in the fact that you fucked that kid's beautiful wife before he did."

Later in the day, Joan buzzed Stone. "Bill Eggers on one." Stone picked up the phone. "Afternoon, Bill."

"Good afternoon, Stone. I just had a call from Benton Blake."

"And how is Benton feeling today?"

"Well, let's see. The court has accepted his financial agreement with Vanessa and issued a decree in their divorce. He's a free man, and he still owns all his real estate, but about fifteen million dollars less in cash. He's still the governor of New York, but he will announce his resignation on Monday, then, after a couple of weeks' holiday, presumably with his new girlfriend, he'll join our firm as a senior partner, so I'd guess he feels pretty good."

"What's he going to do about running for senator?" Stone asked.

"He didn't say."

Fifteen minutes later Joan told him Senator Saltonstall was on the phone.

"Good afternoon, Eliot," Stone said.

"Good afternoon, Stone. Did you watch Peter on TV this morning?"

"I watched his declaration on *Morning Joe,* followed by interviews on half a dozen television shows," Stone replied.

"And what did you think of the impression he made?"

"I thought he came across as handsome, brilliant, and fully qualified for office. I missed only Celeste."

"Funny, that's what I thought, too. Don't worry, you're going to see Celeste on every daytime television show next week, starting Sunday, and in a dozen magazines' next issue. Faith Mackey is doing a superb job."

"I'm delighted to hear all of that."

"Now," Saltonstall said, "tell me if Benton Blake is going to declare for the Senate."

"I have no idea, Eliot," Stone said with some satisfaction, "and I doubt if Benton does, either. We'll just have to wait and see."

# 40

On Monday morning Stone watched on TV as *Morning Joe* switched to a shot of Benton Blake at the governor's desk in Albany.

"Good morning," Blake said, managing a bit of a smile. "I have served New York State as your governor, always with profound gratitude for the support that the citizens and elected officials of this state have given me. Now the time has come for me to move on. I am resigning as governor, effective immediately, and Lieutenant Governor Pio Rinaldi will be sworn in as your new governor in this office in just a few minutes. Pio and I have worked hand in hand for the past years, and I know he will be a governor that you can be proud of.

"I am leaving on a brief vacation, and as soon as I'm back, I will be returning to the private practice of law, with the New York firm of Woodman & Weld. A note to the press and the media — I have already

251

conducted my last press conference as governor, and as a private citizen, I will have nothing further to say.

"I thank everyone who has contributed to the success of my administration and all those around the state who have given me their support. Goodbye and good luck to all of you."

The screen went dark, then returned to *Morning Joe.*

"I have it on good authority," Joe Scarborough said, "that Governor Blake's divorce became final on Friday, and that has freed him to make a new start in life. We wish him well."

Stone's bedside phone rang, and he answered it.

"Stone, it's Eliot Saltonstall."

"Good morning, Eliot," he replied, glancing at the clock. "I didn't know you were up and about at this hour."

"Did you see Benton's announcement?"

"I did."

"I hear he's off to Bermuda with his new girlfriend. I wasn't able to come up with her name."

"I've heard that it's Gloria Parsons, formerly a writer at *Just Folks* magazine."

"Ah! You always know everything, Stone."

"Just something borne in on the Southern breeze."

"Do you think he'll announce for the Senate when he gets back?"

"You just heard him say he'll be joining Woodman & Weld on his return. I don't think Bill Eggers would consider that a good time to make a political announcement."

"Do you think he'll run eventually?"

"I imagine he'll be licking his wounds for some time, after watching Peter's performance on Friday."

"He was good, wasn't he?"

"He certainly was."

"Oh, I received your check for the PAC. I'm very grateful to you, and so is Peter. I expect you'll be hearing from him personally quite soon. Well, if you'll excuse me, I have to get to my office."

"So do I," Stone replied, and they both hung up.

When Stone got to his desk he found a hand-delivered note from Peter Rule, thanking him for his support and promising his friendship forever. "Forever is a couple of weeks in politics," Stone said aloud to himself.

Joan buzzed him. "Bob Cantor to see you."

"Send him in."

Bob came in, was greeted by the other Bob, and took a seat. "I expect you'll want to shut down the wire at Gloria Parsons's place, given Blake's announcement this morning."

"I expect so," Stone said.

"I thought you might like to hear what I've got up to today." Bob set the recorder on the desk and pressed a button.

Stone listened to the recording in full; it was voice-activated, so a few days' conversation was shrunk to a few minutes. "Thank you, Bob," he said. "Give Joan your bill, and we'll wait to see what, if anything, develops when they return from Bermuda."

"I was sort of hoping you'd ask me to follow them there," Bob said.

"Fat chance." The two men shook hands, and Cantor left.

Stone thought about it for a moment, then called Eliot Saltonstall.

"Yes, Stone?"

"I thought you'd like to know — I just spoke to someone who knows Benton Blake well, and I was told that he found Peter's declaration so dispiriting that he has put aside all thought of running for the Senate at midterm."

"That's wonderful news, Stone."

"Apparently Benton said that, instead, he would just wait around for you to have a stroke or something, then run for your seat."

"That's not funny, Stone."

"I thought it was in very poor taste, myself, even if he did say it only privately."

"Well, I had my annual physical last week, and my doctor said I'm fit for at least two more terms."

"I'm sure you are, Eliot, and I'll look forward to voting for you."

"Thank you, Stone."

They hung up.

Gloria Parsons closed her suitcase, had a look out the window for the limo, then made a phone call to Alphonse Teppi.

"How are you, Gloria? It's been a while."

"I've been busy, Al."

"Lunch today?"

"Sorry, I'm going away for a week or so."

"Oh? Where?"

"That's classified. I want you to do something for me while I'm gone."

"Sure thing."

"I want you to put somebody on Stone Barrington. I want to know where he goes and what he does while I'm gone."

"That could get expensive, Gloria."

"I've already told my accountant to send

255

you a nice check. I'll take care of any necessary travel expenses, too."

"Will I be able to reach you?"

"You can text me, and I'll get it — but only if something important comes up."

"I'll get right on it, then. Have a good trip."

"Thank you, Al. I'll call you when I get back."

Her bell rang, and she buzzed the downstairs door open. A minute later there was a knock on the door and a man in a black suit stood there. "May I take your bags, Ms. Parsons?" he asked.

"Right there," she said, pointing at the stack.

Three minutes later she was in the back of the limo, headed for Teterboro and a chartered jet. She snuggled up to Blake. "We're going to make you forget all about politics," she whispered in his ear.

"I'll look forward to forgetting," he said.

## 41

Stone picked up the *New York Times* and read a front-page story to the effect that Benton and Vanessa Blake had amicably agreed to a divorce and that a property settlement fair to both had been reached. Essentially, Vanessa had gotten $15,000,000, plus a house or apartment still to be found, with a value of $5,000,000. Benton had also agreed to a lifetime of child support and school and university fees and support up to and including the Ph.D. level, for their daughter. He then turned on morning TV and found the story featured, but briefly, on every show. The whole thing had been conducted in a businesslike manner, with neither party criticized for his/her actions and attitudes. Step one was over.

Later, Stone encountered a front-page story in the *Times* to the effect that Benton Blake had resigned from the office of governor of New York State, with immediate effect, and that the lieutenant governor, one Pio Rinaldi, heretofore only rarely heard of, had been sworn in as governor.

Five days after that a story ran on the front page of the business section of the *Times,* with a similar story in the *Wall Street Journal,* that Benton Blake had joined the prestigious law firm of Woodman & Weld as a senior partner with responsibility for governmental relations with both Albany and Washington, D.C.

Two days after that a photograph appeared on the front page of the Arts section of the *New York Times* showing the former governor of New York attending a special benefit performance of the musical *Hamilton,* with his companion, Gloria Parsons, the well-known magazine journalist. In the days following, the couple appeared in the collection of tiny photographs taken at three big-time society functions, in a regular *Times* feature that Stone had always thought should have been entitled *Parties That You Weren't Invited To.*

All of the rumors Stone had been privy to had now been enshrined in the political, business, arts, and social annals of the city and state. The social order had been slightly but firmly reordered, and all seemed right with the world.

■ ■ ■ ■

Joan buzzed Stone: "Dino on one."

"Good morning, Commissioner."

"Good morning, prognosticator," Dino said. "That's what one calls a rumormonger whose dirt has been compressed into stone."

"I thank you for the promotion," Stone said.

"All that remains is the political action. When do you reckon that may come to pass?"

"I should think sometime after the New Year, since people wouldn't want these extremely important announcements to become entangled in the *Times*'s holiday collection of Macy's ads, heartwarming stories of how your contributions have given many disadvantaged families a hopeful holiday season, and stories of how members of Congress are spending their generous Christmas recesses, at home, serving their constituencies."

"So I shouldn't worry about that until, what, Super Bowl time?"

"Just a guess," Stone said. "Maybe just after or in conjunction with the presidential inauguration, on January twentieth, after, of course, the incumbent has sorrowfully announced his intention not to seek reelection, in order to spend more time with his family."

"This should make the conversation on our upcoming warm-weather cruise."

"It's good of you to call it that, since speaking the location over the telephone might broadcast it to all the wrong people. The White House has made no announcement of its inhabitants' holiday plans, as yet. I expect the secretary will sneak it into a press room briefing at some point, surrounded by statements about more important or more exciting events."

"What should Viv and I bring along in the way of clothing for this outing?"

"One or more bathing suits, of course, in the case of Viv, revealing ones, and the usual assortment of colorful cruise wear. Our guest of honor has requested, through her secretary of state, that gentlemen should also bring a business suit and a dinner suit, for some special occasion as yet unrevealed."

"I take it 'dinner suit,' to us hoi polloi, means 'tuxedo.' "

"You may assume that. You may also substitute appropriate naval or yachting formal wear, should you possess same."

"I take that to mean that you possess such finery."

"I and perhaps others. Ladies to dress appropriately, of course."

"What does that mean?"

"Your wife will know."

"How is our guest of honor planning to deal with her absence from her usual residence?"

"I can't tell you that on the phone, only over dinner."

"Patroon, at seven?"

"Done."

At Patroon, after a first drink, Dino raised the subject not mentionable on the phone.

"This is how it's going to go," Stone said, "but it's only a plan and can change."

"Shoot," Dino said.

Stone outlined the security precautions as he imagined they would be.

"Jesus," Dino said when he had finished, "are they really that worried about our safety?"

"No, Dino, they are entirely concerned with the health and well-being of the people they are charged with protecting. I very much doubt whether they care if we live or die."

"That's not very comforting," Dino replied.

"Perhaps it will comfort you to think that, if some attempt is made on the welfare of the people they are charged with protecting, they will have to protect us in order to protect them."

"I'm a little less uncomfortable with that."

"Then perhaps you should arrange for a platoon of New York Police Department personnel to charter another yacht and accompany us, with an eye toward saving your ass, in the event that an attack is made on our guests."

"That's not a bad idea," Dino said. "I'll give it some thought."

# 42

Peter Rule parked his car in the Capitol garage, went to the Russell building, entered Senator Eliot Saltonstall's office, and took a seat.

"I spoke earlier this morning with a reliable source," Saltonstall said, "and there's news of Benton Blake."

"Oh?"

"He's off to Bermuda for a week or two with his new girlfriend, Gloria Parsons."

"Isn't she the one Stone had thrown out of our wedding reception?"

"One and the same."

"Interesting that she's with Blake. How long?"

"My impression is very recently. My source also tells me that Blake was upset by your announcement, and he won't be declaring for the Senate."

"He's just depressed, he'll get over it."

"He was actually quoted as saying he

would just wait around for me to have a stroke, then run for my seat."

"How rude of him."

"I thought so, too."

"How did your physical go, Senator?"

"I'm tip-top."

Peter watched the senator blink rapidly and immediately knew he was lying. He never played poker with the senator because the tell made him too easy to read. "My guess is Blake's impatience will outrun his depression. We should expect him to run later. In the meantime, I have to run as though I'm already behind."

"You'll want to get commitments from as many state and party officials as you can. We don't know what other candidates will arise in the meantime. Faith Mackey is working on a plan to keep you in the news. If we can make you look like a foregone conclusion, other potential candidates may wither on the vine."

"Wither on the vine," Peter repeated. "I like the sound of that, Senator."

"Peter, you're my son-in-law now, you can call me Dad."

"I already have two dads to refer to, it could get confusing."

"Call me Eliot, then? I'd like that."

"Henceforth you are Eliot," Peter said.

"Anything else this morning?"

"Not that I can think of."

"Then I'd better start working the phones," Peter said.

"Who will you be calling?"

"I've got a long list."

"Get to it, then," Saltonstall said, making shooing motions.

"Good morning, Eliot." Peter left and went back to his office. It was larger than that of most chiefs of staff in the Senate because his senator had more seniority than most. He had room for a sofa and a couple of easy chairs, and there were paintings of the Hudson Valley School on the walls and books of an appropriate nature: the three Roosevelts — Teddy, Franklin, and Eleanor — and an array of Kennedys, plus biographies. Republicans were not represented. His private line rang, and he picked it up. No one unimportant to him had that number.

"Hello."

"Mr. Rule, will you speak to the President?"

"I suppose so," Peter drawled.

There was a click. "It's your ma," she said.

"Hello, Ma."

"Don't call me that — only I can call me Ma."

"Hello, Mudder."

"You are exasperating, but you handled your announcement beautifully."

"Thank you, my dear."

"Your voice is always deeper when you're speaking to groups. It reminds me of my father."

"That's high praise."

"Word has reached me that Benton Blake will not be running against you."

"That word has reached me, too, but it's not in my interests to believe it, not until the polls have closed, anyway."

"You're my wisest son," she said.

"That's not especially high praise since Billy is only four. Are you bringing him on the cruise?"

"He doesn't want to go, if you can believe that. He's afraid he'll be seasick."

"Has he ever been seasick?"

"No, he just heard about it somewhere. We're dropping him off in Georgia. Aunt Bee will stay with him. He always gets excited about the cows and horses, and he wants to visit his pony."

"You never got me a pony," he said reprovingly.

"You were an urban child — you couldn't have a pony in Georgetown."

"I suppose you're right, but I still resent it."

"If that's all you resent, then I must have been a very good mother."

"You were a very good mother because you were too busy to interfere very much in my life. I liked making my own decisions."

"That's true, you always have. That's a character trait that will stand you in good stead in politics."

"All I have to do is imitate you and Will."

"Oh, thank you for that!"

"Listen, don't you have a country to run?"

"Oops, forgot about that. I'm out of here." They both hung up.

Peter ran over the list of calls on his desk and found the most important one missing. He called the office of the senior senator from New York and asked for his chief of staff, Dick Porter. "Tell him it's the putative junior senator from New York."

"Porter."

"Hey, Dick."

"How you doing?"

"I'm hungry. Let's have lunch."

"See you in an hour."

They met in the Senate dining room, in which their staff status allowed them to lunch, and Peter wangled a corner table.

"Congrats," Dick said. He was fifteen years older than Peter, and shorter.

"Thanks, Dick."

They ordered quickly out of habit and had iced tea instead of wine.

"What's happening?" Dick asked.

"It has come to my attention that you are going to become unemployed next year."

"So kind of you to mention it."

"It's best to inject a little anxiety into a conversation like this one."

"What kind of conversation is this?"

"One where I ease your fears of unemployment."

"Ease away, pal."

"Dick, you have the reputation of being the best chief of staff on the Hill."

Dick grinned. "I've heard that, and I can't bring myself to disagree."

"Do you like the work?"

"The only thing I'd like better is my senator's job, but I'm ill-suited for that by temperament and intellect."

"You mean, you're smarter than your boss."

"Ah, you know how I feel."

"How'd you like to keep your job for, say, another two terms, maybe three?"

"You mean my guy is going to stand for reelection?"

"No, I don't."

"Then who in the world is going to replace him who would keep me on the payroll?"

"It ain't going to be Benton Blake," Peter said.

"Ah, then it must be you."

"Right, and I'd like you to come work for me."

"After Election Day?"

"Today, if you like."

"And walk out on my senator?"

"You've never liked him all that much. It's hard working for someone dumber than you, so working for me should be a refreshing change."

"Where's my office going to be, if I walk out on my man?"

"In my house in Georgetown, with a direct line to my desk here, until I'm running full-time. And you can spend the summer at my place in the Hamptons, if you like. The phones work between here and there, so it wouldn't be much different than having you in Georgetown."

"My wife would like that."

"Is she pregnant yet?"

"No, and her doctor says that's not really in the cards."

"I'm sorry."

"Don't be. I'd make a lousy father."

"I'll pay you half again what you're making now, and double what you're making when the campaign starts. After I'm in office, I'll supplement your government salary handsomely."

"You say all the right words, Peter."

"How about these words — start the day after New Year's Day, that will give you time to break the news gently to your boss."

"Not a problem. I've been grooming my deputy for a couple of years — she can take over."

Peter held out his hand. "Welcome aboard."

Dick shook and held it. "You know, I think I'd make a great White House chief of staff."

"All in good time," Peter said.

## 43

Stone Barrington got out of the Bentley at Bergdorf's and began to tour the shops on the way downtown. He found a lovely cashmere dressing gown for Holly, and a sweater for Joan at Saks. He strolled over to Rockefeller Center and had a close-up look at the big tree.

He was standing in front of a shoe store, examining their display, as if he needed more shoes, when he caught a glimpse of the reflection of a familiar figure in the plate-glass window, but before he could turn around, the crowd of tourists surged, and the figure disappeared. What the hell, he thought, he'd lived in this city his whole life, and it would be unusual not to run into someone he knew, even if he couldn't figure out who.

Alphonse Teppi took a tweed hat from his coat pocket and pulled it on, then donned his glasses. He thought Barrington had spotted him, but he seemed safe now.

Benton Blake and Gloria Parsons strolled along a pink beach in Bermuda, hand in hand. The sand made squeaking sounds as they walked. Benton was wearing a Panama hat and sunglasses; he didn't want to be recognized and photographed with a woman at an intimate resort so soon after his divorce.

"Listen," Gloria said, "if you're not going to run for anything, what the hell do you care if you're seen with me?"

"I'm still a politician," Benton said, "and we think about those things. I've had years of being cautious about where I'm seen and with whom, and it doesn't go away immediately after a divorce decree. It's a reflex. It's one thing to be seen together at a party or the theater, another to get caught shacking up in Bermuda."

"Okay, I get it," Gloria said. Her phone rang. "Excuse me a minute. Hello?"

"Hey, it's Al."

"Hey."

"I'm on Barrington, like you asked, but it's really boring."

"Gee, I'm sorry about that. You didn't ask for boredom money. What's he doing?"

"He's walking around Rockefeller Center,

gawking at the tree and the skaters like somebody from Wichita, or something."

"Most people are boring most of the time, Al."

"Oh, all right, I'll stay on him." He hung up.

"What was that about?" Benton asked.

"Oh, it's nothing, just an acquaintance who was bored and wanted to talk to somebody."

"In New York?"

"Yes."

"What's the weather like there?"

"Cold and sunny, according to the forecast on TV this morning."

"I'm glad to hear it, otherwise, why come to Bermuda?"

Stone went into a wine shop and found a very expensive bottle of vintage cognac for Dino, then he went into the Diamond Center and found a lovely broach for Viv. He couldn't find anybody following him, but neither could he shake the feeling that somebody was out there.

Teppi got Danny Blaine on the phone. "What time do you get off work?"

"At five, like everybody else, unless I work late."

"I'll need you to spell me shortly after five. I didn't dress for the weather, and I'm freezing my ass off."

"So, you want me to freeze *my* ass off, is that it?"

"You've got a sheepskin coat, darling, and you're young and hardy, unlike me."

"All right, where do you want me to meet you?"

"Right now he's in the Diamond Center, on Fifth at Forty-seventh Street, and he seems to generally be heading downtown." He looked at his watch. "It's four-thirty now, so he ought to be in your neighborhood around five, if he keeps this slow pace."

"I'll call you when I'm leaving my building."

"Great." Teppi hung up and stamped his feet, trying to get some circulation going. He looked up to see Barrington coming out of the Diamond Center, talking on his phone. Teppi turned his back and pulled the hat down over his forehead, watching Barrington's reflection in a shop window. He was just standing on the corner, looking uptown.

This went on while Teppi kept stamping his feet. Then a green Bentley turned a corner and pulled up to where Barrington stood, and he got in and was driven away.

"Shit!" Teppi said aloud, and started waving his arms for a taxi. The Bentley turned a corner and glided out of sight. Teppi's phone rang.

"Okay, I got out of the office early," Danny said. "Where are you?"

"Never mind," Teppi said, "he got into his Bentley and drove away, and there are no vacant cabs on Fifth Avenue."

"Do you know where he's going?"

"Probably home. You know the address — take a cab over there and see if he's home. If he is, he won't be going out for dinner until seven or so."

"Tell me again why we're doing this," Danny said.

"Because Gloria wants it, that's why. I can never say no to her, and neither can you. She got you out of the jug, didn't she?"

"Oh, all right, I'll get over there. Here comes a cab!"

Stone walked into Joan's office. "I know this is weird," he said, "but I can't shake the feeling that I'm being followed." He looked out the window but saw nobody.

"Paranoia does not become you," Joan replied, then went back to her work.

Stone sat down at his desk and went

through his phone messages, then returned some calls.

A few minutes later Joan buzzed him.

"Yes?"

"You're being followed," she said. "Come in here."

Stone went into her office.

"Look out there," she said, pointing to the window.

Stone looked out and saw a thin, fashionable-looking young man leaning against a tree across the street and smoking a cigarette.

"He got out of a cab ten minutes ago," Joan said.

"I've never seen him before," Stone replied.

"Why do you think he's following you?"

"If I don't know him, how would I know why he's following me?"

"I guess that makes a weird kind of sense."

"It makes perfect sense," Stone said.

"You want me to take a shot at him?" Joan asked.

"Not yet," Stone replied. He walked out of her office, stepped out the front door, and yelled, "Hey!"

The young man jerked to attention.

"What do you want?"

He threw away his cigarette and sprinted

toward Third Avenue.

Stone thought he was remarkably fast. He went back inside and found Joan standing at the window.

"Maybe you're not paranoid," she said.

# 44

On the appointed date, Stone had Fred drive him to Teterboro Airport, where he did a thorough preflight inspection on his Citation CJ3 Plus, ran through his checklist, and started the engines. He received a clearance as filed. It seemed that there must be little traffic; everyone was home for the holidays.

He took off for Manassas; the air traffic controllers sounded bored, and he heard little chat on the radios. He received a vector of direct Manassas, landed there after an hour's flight, and taxied to the FBO ramp. Holly, Peter, and Celeste came out of the building and pushed a cart toward the airplane as he cut the engines.

Stone loaded their luggage, made Peter and Celeste comfortable in the passenger seats, and invited Holly to fly right seat. She was a licensed pilot and could work the radios for him. Fifteen minutes later they were climbing toward forty thousand feet and winging their way toward Key West.

At almost the same moment, a Gulfstream jet took off from Andrews Air Force Base.

Billy Lee sat next to his mother, reading *Lassie Come Home.*

"How's the book?" she asked.

"The dog is dragging through a swamp with a broken leg," he replied.

"Don't worry, he'll get better," she replied.

"Don't tell me the ending!"

She raised her hands in surrender.

"Mom," Billy said, looking around, "this isn't Air Force One."

"Yes, it is," she replied.

"No, it isn't. Air Force One is a lot bigger and has a lot of people on it."

"It's like this, sweetheart — whatever airplane the President is flying on is called Air Force One — big or small. It's what's called a radio call sign."

"Oh," Billy replied, and added another fact to the growing collection in his young brain.

Two hours later, the Gulfstream set down at Warm Springs, Georgia, where the runway had been lengthened to accommodate big jets when Will Lee had been President.

Three SUVs rolled up to the airplane, and two Secret Service agents who resembled the Lees got out. They walked down the airstair, waving at the little knot of media behind a fence a hundred yards away, and the SUV's door closed behind them. Billy understood the ruse, and he knew that he was spending his vacation in Georgia with his pony and his aunt Bee.

The airplane taxied to the end of the runway and took off. Its radio call sign was still Air Force One.

Stone set down the CJ3 at Key West International at dusk and taxied to the ramp, where a van waited to receive them and their luggage. Once in the van, Stone asked to be taken to the U.S. Coast Guard installation in Key West Harbor. "Everybody brought their passports, as requested, right?"

He got an affirmative noise from the group.

"Give them to me, please."

After a ten-minute drive they reached the gate of the base. Stone handed the passports to the uniformed guard and they were admitted. He dealt out the passports to their owners.

*Breeze,* wearing the British White Ensign,

was docked next to a smaller yacht, *Scout,* in what had been the old Key West submarine base, now occupied by the Coast Guard. A Secret Service agent checked their passports, and the crew carried their luggage aboard and settled them in their cabins. After unpacking, they met in the yacht's saloon for a drink.

Stone raised his glass. "Welcome aboard," he said, and everybody drank. "Let me explain exactly what's going on," he said.

"Please do," Peter said. "This is all very mysterious. To begin with, why is the yacht flying the British White Ensign? I thought that was the exclusive right of Royal Navy ships."

"If you had seen the stern you would have learned that *Breeze* is now called *Trafalgar III.* She is now carried on *Lloyd's List* as a British-registered vessel owned by the commodore of the Royal Yacht Squadron, the British members of which are also allowed to fly the White Ensign. Foreigners like me are also allowed to fly it, as long as their vessels are registered in Britain, which we now are — temporarily. We're also flying the Squadron's burgee, which is a triangular version of the White Ensign.

"Kate and Will's flight is timed to land after dark, just about now, at the Key West

Naval Air Station. They dropped off Billy in Georgia earlier."

"Why all the secrecy?" Celeste asked.

"They just don't want to attract attention while on vacation," Stone said.

As he spoke, Air Force One set down at the Naval Air Station, on Boca Chica Island, a few miles away. From the ramp the aircraft was towed into a large hangar, and the Lees disembarked there and were driven to the Coast Guard base. They were welcomed aboard by the rest of their party, and after they had settled into the owner's suite, they joined the others for a drink. The yacht's engines started.

As their arrival was toasted, the yacht moved slowly into the main channel and, followed by the smaller vessel, left Key West under a bright moon.

"We're going to anchor off one of the smaller islands," Stone said, "in order to attract as little attention as possible. The other yacht is carrying Secret Service and other support personnel and some communications equipment that goes everywhere with the President."

An hour later, they anchored and were soon called to dinner.

"I apologize for all the secrecy," Kate said

to the party, "but we didn't want to be hounded by the press on this cruise."

"We quite understand," Stone replied.

The captain appeared to greet them. "I thought you'd like to know that the radio traffic in Key West Harbor was all about the British yacht. They seem to think that there's a high British official aboard or maybe a rock star. When you wake up tomorrow morning we will already be under way, and our destination will be Fort Jefferson, a pre–Civil War fort in the island group called the Dry Tortugas, about sixty or seventy miles west of Key West."

Later, in their cabin, Stone gave Holly her Christmas gift. "I thought you might want to wear it on our cruise."

Holly slipped the cashmere robe over her naked body. "What do you think?" she asked, modeling it for him.

"A perfect fit. I think it looks great on you, but I prefer the earlier, more naked version."

They fell asleep in each other's arms.

## 45

Gloria was dropped off by Benton Blake at her apartment, and the chauffeur carried her bags upstairs. The Bermuda trip had gone off without a hitch, and they had decided to go back there to be married.

As she was unpacking, her phone rang. "Hello?"

"Oh, thank God you're back," Hazel, her editor at *Just Folks,* said. "I've got an assignment for you."

"Oh, Hazel, I just got in."

"What, you no longer need the money? I'll give you five grand for the piece and pay your travel expenses to Key West."

"Key West? In the dead of winter? You bet your ass I'll do it. I can keep up my new tan!"

"All right, I'll see if we can buy a seat on a charter jet. Oh, and pick a photographer and tell him to bring some long lenses. We've chartered a little boat that you two can live on and use to chase the big boat. Got a pencil?"

"Always."

"Okay, the yacht you're chasing is called *Trafalgar III,* and she belongs to the commodore of the Royal Yacht Squadron, who's not aboard. That means there's a big fish to catch, maybe even the prime minister, or at the very least a movie or rock star. He wouldn't lend his yacht to just anybody."

"Good deal." She wasn't going to see Benton for a week or so, anyway; he had a lot to do, and the press would be paying too much attention. "Let me know when my flight leaves." Gloria stopped unpacking and started repacking. Fortunately, her Bermuda wardrobe would do just fine for Key West.

She called a British photographer friend, Robert Marks. "Hey, Bobby, would you like a week in a warm place?"

"Depends which warm place."

"Key West and environs."

"What are we shooting?"

"A fugitive celebrity — bring your longest lenses."

"When are we leaving?"

"Today, very shortly. Pack and wait for my call. Travel is first-class all the way, and we'll be living aboard a yacht."

"Can I bring a girl?"

"Absolutely not — it's just you, me, and the crew."

"Oh, hell, all right."

"I'll call you when I know the time, so be ready."

"Righto."

She hung up and continued packing. Her phone rang. "Yeah?"

"I got you seats on a Challenger. Be at Atlantic Aviation, Teterboro, at three PM sharp, with your seat belt buckled. I'll send a car for you at one-thirty."

"Gotcha."

"And bring your passports to identify yourselves to the charter company."

"Gotcha."

"Call me with news."

"Gotcha." She called her photographer and told him to bring his passport.

"It's stitched to my arm," he said.

"I'll pick you up at one forty-five."

"Done."

She closed her bags and called Benton, glancing at her watch: 1:15.

"Yes?"

"Hey, hon, I've got an assignment in Key West, car's coming in fifteen minutes."

"How long?"

"A week, maybe."

"Call me when you arrive, so I'll know

you're safe. Love you."

"Love you, too." She hung up.

At 3:30 PM she and Marks were buckled into their seats, she clutching an envelope with the charter boat papers inside. A hedge-fund manager and his girlfriend sat opposite them, holding hands. They offered only first names by way of introduction, Gary and Sheree. Gloria looked them over. He's married, she said to herself, and not to her.

Just after dark they landed at Key West International and took a cab to the Galleon Marina, where they found the berth number. Her name was *Ciao,* and she was glorious: fifty feet, very nice condition, two nice cabins, a couple to skipper and feed them.

Captain Hal and his wife, Judy, offered them a drink and sat down. "So," he said, "where would you like to go?"

"There's a yacht called *Trafalgar III,* flying a British flag," Gloria said. "We want to go wherever she goes, but we don't want to crowd them."

Captain Hal's eyebrows shot up. "Come with me," he said.

Gloria and Bobby followed him on deck, where Captain Hal stood and pointed.

"There she is."

*Trafalgar III* was steaming past them fifty yards away, in the main channel.

Gloria gaped, while Bobby snapped. "Follow that yacht!" she said, clapping her hands and jumping up and down.

Stone woke early, only shortly after dawn. He pulled back the curtain over the port next to their bed, and a big red ball was rising out of the sea.

"What's up?" Holly asked sleepily.

"Sun's coming up."

"Happens every day."

"Not like this. Come see."

She came and stood next to him. "Wow."

"How about a morning dip?"

"I'm on."

"Nobody's up — be bold."

They went aft, to the fantail. Wearing only robes.

A steward stood there holding a silver tray bearing two Bloody Marys.

"You're up early," Holly said. "Oh, what the hell." She grabbed one. "I'm on vacation."

They drank them hurriedly, then went and stood near the aft rail. "Ready?" he asked.

"Ready."

They shed their robes and dove in, then

288

came up shouting. "The water's perfect!" Stone yelled.

A couple of hundred yards away *Ciao* swung at anchor, and Bobby Marks was pointing a camera at the swimmers, with a lens that looked like a cannon. Gloria peeked out of the main companionway. "What's going on?"

"Life has showed itself," he said, snapping away.

Gloria looked up just in time to see a man and a woman climbing up a ladder, then diving off the fantail of *Trafalgar III*. She squinted at them.

"Anybody we know?"

"Let me see what you shot."

He turned the electronic camera so she could see the screen. "Zoom in," she said. "Let's get a look at their faces."

He did so. "Great resolution, isn't it?"

Gloria put her glasses on and looked at the camera. "Holy shit!"

"What's wrong?"

"The guy is named Stone Barrington, from New York. The woman is our celebrity — Holly Barker, the fucking secretary of state!"

"Holy shit!" Bobby said, taking more pictures.

# 46

As Gloria watched, two other naked people stood on the fantail and dived off with a shriek.

"Are you getting this?" she asked Bobby.

"Every bit of it," Bobby replied, snapping away.

"Let me see their faces."

Bobby showed her the display and zoomed in.

"Holy shit!"

"Who is it this time?"

"It's the daughter of Senator Eliot Saltonstall and the son of the fucking President of the United States!"

"Holy shit," Bobby said, taking shots of them climbing the ladder for another dive.

"The only thing better than this would be if the two presidents are aboard."

"That would be pushing our luck," Bobby said.

"Are you getting a Wi-Fi signal out here?"

Bobby checked his phone. "Nope, no Wi-Fi, no cell service."

"Shit, shit, shit! I wanted to send these to Hazel. I can't even call her!"

"Hey," Bobby said, "*Trafalgar III* is weighing anchor."

"Let's get inside," Gloria said, "I don't want to be seen when they pass." They dived into the saloon.

Stone, Holly, Peter, and Celeste sat in the fantail, laughing and toweling their hair. Another tray of Bloody Marys arrived.

"That was fantastic!" Celeste enthused. "We have to start every day that way."

"You talked me into it," Stone said, taking a sip from his drink. "Make my next one a Bloody Awful," Stone said to the crewman.

"What's that, sir?"

"No vodka."

Kate Lee appeared in the doorway to the saloon, took one look and retreated. "Who's that?" she shouted, pointing. They were steaming past *Ciao*.

"Just another yacht," Stone replied. "They were anchored some distance from us last night."

Kate waited until *Ciao* was well astern before emerging. She waved away a Bloody Mary. "Make it a Virgin Mary," she said.

"It's called a Bloody Awful," Stone said.

"A better name. You never know when I might have to deal with the Russians, so I'll be drinking very little on this voyage."

"I will be," Will said, emerging from the saloon and grabbing a Bloody Mary. "I'm not dealing with the Russians or anybody else, for that matter, and I don't have to drive a car or tend a four-year-old." He took a swig. "God, I haven't had a Bloody Mary for years! It's wonderful!"

A buffet was quickly set up, containing scrambled eggs, bacon and sausages, and pancakes, with assorted muffins and breads. Everybody dug in.

Stone picked up a large pair of binoculars and scanned the area aft. *Ciao* was weighing anchor, well behind their support yacht, *Scout.* "We must have woken them up," he said.

They steamed west at a leisurely eight knots until late in the afternoon, when Fort Jefferson hove into view. The yacht followed the buoys around the island, and they entered the lagoon with the fort on their port side. They picked up a mooring, and the crew put out a stern anchor from a dinghy to hold the big yacht in place without swinging. Half an hour later *Scout* came into the lagoon and anchored in the same way, perhaps forty yards away. Shortly, her tender departed and came over to *Trafalgar III,* then four people in nautical gear came aboard.

The captain came aft to say good evening. "Some people from *Scout* are doing a communications check aboard, with the radio they installed, and the Secret Service are changing shifts. The others will be going back to *Scout* soon. By the way, although there's no cellular service out here, we have a working satphone, and there's a handset in the saloon, if anyone needs to make a call. You dial zero-one-one, then the area code, then the number, then press 'enter.' " He went back to his duties.

Kate finished her drink and looked at her watch. "I'd better call Billy and see how he's making out." She left the group and went into the saloon.

"I can tell you," Will said to the others, "Billy is doing just fine. He'd bring that pony into the family quarters at the White House if we'd let him."

Cocktails were served a little later, and they watched the sun sink into the sea.

*Ciao* was anchored outside the lagoon, on the leeward side of the island. Gloria watched *Trafalgar III* through a pair of ten-power binoculars. "Can't see much," she said to Bobby. "And they've got a stern anchor out, so they're not going to swing around and give us a view from aft."

"Gee, I guess I'll have to take the rest of the day off," Bobby said, accepting a drink from Judy, then handing Gloria one. "We haven't had time to catch up," he said. "What have you been up to?"

"Just between you and me?"

"Absolutely."

"I've been in Bermuda for a week with Benton Blake."

"Our ex-governor?"

"One and the same."

"He's not wasting any time after his divorce, is he?"

"Nor before it. We're going to be married a little way down the road."

"I wish you every happiness," he said. "What's the guv going to do for a living?"

"He's joining the big-time law firm of Woodman & Weld as a senior partner."

"Well, that should keep you both in fish and chips."

"In champagne and caviar," she replied.

"I should have expected no less," he replied. "You've always had an eye for the main chance."

" 'Main chance,' " Gloria repeated. "I like the sound of that. Benton is certainly the main chance for me, and I for him. He hasn't been happy for a long time, and he deserves what I can give him."

"And I well know what that is," Bobby said.

"You certainly do," she replied, "and if you play your cards right, you might have the opportunity on this cruise."

He raised his glass. "I'll look forward to it."

"So will I," she replied. After all, she had never been a one-man woman, and she couldn't see herself starting now, on a cruise like this, not with an old flame aboard.

## 47

The following morning, Stone woke at
dawn again, nudged Holly, then put on a
robe and walked to the fantail and looked
around; the only yacht in the lagoon was
*Scout.* He could see the outline of *Ciao,* the
smaller yacht from the day before, anchored
off in the lee of the island.

"I'm not stripping off," Holly said. "That
other yacht is full of horny Secret Service
guys, and they're not getting a peek."

"Then go put on something skimpy and
bring me a suit, too," Stone said. "I'll wait
impatiently."

Holly went below and returned quickly.
"Let's do it."

They dropped their robes, Stone put on
the suit, and in a moment they were in the
water. Stone stroked out a few yards from
*Trafalgar III,* then, facedown in the water, he
saw a very large, dark shape on the bottom,
shark-shaped, and, he reckoned, twelve to

fifteen feet. He reversed course.

"Follow me," he said, as he reached Holly, "and don't ask questions." He escorted her to the ladder, and they climbed aboard.

"What was that about?" Holly asked.

"Very large shark on the bottom," he replied.

"Oops." A crewman bearing their Bloody Marys approached. "Not to worry," he said, "that's a nurse shark. They spend most of their time on the bottom, and the only danger is stepping on one."

"Hold those drinks," Stone said, grabbing Holly's hand and jumping back into the water.

"Where is it?" she asked.

"That way," he said, pointing.

She ducked under the water for half a minute, then emerged. "It's not moving," she said.

"Nurse shark," he replied. "The only danger is stepping on it."

"Gosh, you know everything, don't you?"

"Nearly everything."

They frolicked in the water for another twenty minutes, then climbed back aboard and found their robes. Bloody Marys in hand, they greeted their fellow cruisers. Peter and Celeste dropped their robes.

"Large nurse shark over there," Stone

said, pointing. "It won't be interested in you, unless you step on it."

"Stone knows everything," Holly said.

"Nearly everything," Stone added.

They dove into the water. By the time they returned, Will and Kate had joined them for breakfast.

"Haven't I been here before?" Kate asked, "and with the same people?"

"Nurse shark over there on the bottom," Stone said. "It won't bother you unless you step on it."

"It seems to me I've heard this song before," Holly said.

"Stone knows everything, doesn't he?" Kate asked.

"Nearly," she replied.

After breakfast Stone and Holly went back to their cabin and showered together, then got interested in each other. When they had made love for a while, they both fell asleep and didn't wake until nearly lunchtime.

"So, is this our routine?" Holly asked. "Swim, eat, fuck, sleep?"

"Then start over," Stone said. "It's all there is to do."

"I brought a book."

"Good luck with getting it read."

■ ■ ■ ■

After lunch and a nap, Kate said, "Will and I are taking the tender over to Loggerhead Key." She pointed. "I hear it has the best beach in the world, and there's nobody there."

"Want some company?" Stone asked.

"Nope," she replied. "And we're taking only one agent." She pointed at a young woman standing by. "You. Can you drive a boat?"

"Yes, ma'am," she replied.

"Then get one in the water, please, and we'll leave."

The only thing on the island was a lighthouse, way down the beach. "You remain here," Kate said to the agent, "and turn your back. We're going to take a walk, and we'll whistle if we need you."

"Ah, ma'am . . ."

"Stay here with your back turned, or I'll have you shot," Kate said firmly.

"Yes, ma'am."

Kate and Will tossed their robes and swimsuits into the boat and, hand in hand and quite naked, they began their stroll up the beach.

The agent stood, uncomfortably, looking away from them.

Aboard *Ciao,* Bobby Marks was watching through his longest lens. "Two people have left the big yacht," he said, "and they're naked. They've gone to Loggerhead Key, over there." He handed Gloria the camera, and she looked.

"I think it's Stone and Holly again," she said, handing him back the camera.

"No, this guy's not as tall as Stone."

"Okay, take some pictures."

Bobby snapped away.

They passed a clump of bushes with a palm in the middle, and Kate dropped to her knees in the sand and held out her arms. "Come to me, Mr. President," she said.

He came to her. "Gee, that's what you used to call me."

"It always turned you on," she said, and they fell into each other's arms.

"The couple went behind some bushes and didn't come out," Bobby said.

"You think they're fucking?"

"There's nothing else to do on that island," he replied.

"Well, the magazine's not going to run

pictures of people fucking, no matter who they are."

"So I can have a drink and take a nap, then?"

"Why not, it'll be my watch for a while."

Bobby snagged a rum and tonic and stretched out on a sofa in the saloon. Soon, he was snoring gently.

Gloria picked up his camera, sighted in the clump of bushes, and focused. The couple must still be at it, she thought. She sat down on a chaise and put the back down. Soon she was sleeping, too.

Kate and Will emerged from behind the bushes and strolled back toward the yacht's tender, dusting off the sand on their bodies. The agent was sitting on the sand, wearing a straw hat, but her back was still to them.

"Don't move," Kate called out. She retrieved their suits and robes, and they dressed.

"Okay," Kate said, "back to the yacht."

The agent waited for them to get in, then shoved the boat free of the sand, got in, and started the engine.

Kate put on a straw hat and her sunglasses, and Will put on a baseball cap.

Gloria was awake again, and she saw the

301

people returning in the boat. She looked through the camera.

Bobby approached her from the saloon. "Who are they?"

"Beats me," she said. "Just some other couple from their party, I guess. Of no interest."

# 48

At lunch, Kate suddenly said, "I like it here. I don't want to go anywhere else until nearly the end of our cruise."

"I think this is the most interesting place we could go," Stone said. "We should probably visit the fort and take the tour."

"This is where Dr. Samuel Mudd was imprisoned, isn't it? After setting John Wilkes Booth's broken leg after the assassination?"

"It is," Stone replied, "and he became a hero after putting down an epidemic of yellow fever on the island."

"I'll have the Secret Service arrange a tour, at a time when there aren't many people there."

"I should think we could go whenever you like — everybody is pretty much home for the holidays."

"Oh, Stone," Kate said, "I forgot to mention that on our next-to-last night, I've arranged something special for us. It's a secret."

"I'll look forward to it, whatever it is."

"I promise you, it will be a memorable occasion."

They spent a lazy week, doing all the things Holly had enumerated. They also watched a couple of movies on DVDs, played charades, and indulged in some card games and chess.

On their fifth night aboard, they went to bed late, and everyone slept soundly. In the middle of the night Stone woke to hear the engines starting. Probably charging batteries, he thought, then he fell soundly asleep again.

He woke to a slight motion of the boat, got up and looked out a porthole. All he saw was sunlight on a calm sea. They appeared to be moving faster than on the trip out.

"What are you doing?" Holly asked.

"We're moving," he said. "This must be Kate's surprise."

"Come back to bed," she said huskily, and he did.

Gloria woke shortly after dawn, got into her swimsuit, and went on deck. It took her a moment to realize that *Trafalgar III* was gone. She ran to the pilothouse and found the captain drinking a cup of coffee. "Where's *Trafalgar III*?" she demanded.

"Over there in the lagoon," he said.

"She's not, she's gone."

The captain had a look. "You're right."

"Where?"

He switched on the radar. "There," he said, pointing at a blip. "She's about twenty miles out, and she'll be off our radar in a moment." With that, the blip disappeared.

"Which direction?"

"South, more or less."

"Get this thing started and follow her," Gloria said.

Judy entered the wheelhouse with the captain's breakfast. "What's going on?"

"We're weighing anchor," the captain said. "*Trafalgar III* is headed south, and we're going to catch her."

"South? There's nothing out there."

"Get on deck and stow the anchor," the captain said, starting the engines and pressing the switch for the windlass that raised the anchor.

Fifteen minutes later they were headed south at twenty-five knots. "We can't keep this speed for more than an hour or two," the captain said to Gloria.

"Why not?"

"Because she uses more than twice the fuel at this speed than at our normal cruise. We want to be able to get home."

An hour and a half later the captain pointed at the radar. "There she is," he said, slowing down. "We can keep her in sight on the scope, but we can't follow her all the way."

"Why not?" Gloria asked.

"Because we don't have the paperwork to arrive legally in Cuba."

*"Cuba?"*

"They're headed directly for Havana."

"Why the hell would they go to Havana?"

"Beats me. Look, we've got a second blip. The nearest one must be *Scout,* and the bigger blip is *Trafalgar III.* Ah, I get it now — the British don't have the same restrictions as we do, with regard to Cuba." He pointed at the radar. "Ship to our east," he said, picking up the binoculars. "Coast Guard cutter," he said, "on the same course as the yachts. Beyond that, visible on radar, is something bigger, maybe a Navy destroyer."

"Are they being chased? Drugs, or something?"

"They appear to be keeping pace, but on the yachts' course, at a distance of about ten miles."

"This gets weirder and weirder," Gloria said.

"Maybe not," Bobby chimed in; he had just entered the wheelhouse.

"Why not?"

"If we're right, and there's some British dignitary on board *Trafalgar III,* maybe the Coast Guard and the Navy are playing the mother hen."

"How far can we follow them?" Gloria asked.

"I don't want to get any closer than thirty miles from Havana. The legal border is the twelve-mile line, but the Cubans have been known to treat that loosely. I don't want a shot across our bows from some patrol boat."

"Well, shit!" Gloria said.

Stone and Holly surfaced for breakfast and were joined by the others.

"Don't ask questions," Holly whispered to him.

"Why not?"

"Kate told you — it's a secret."

"We appear to be headed for South America," Stone said.

"Relax, and enjoy the ride."

Kate and Will joined them. "We'll be having guests for lunch," she said. "I've spoken to the captain about that. We may need to lunch from a buffet."

Stone didn't ask questions, but he knew their table would seat twelve. Who was coming aboard?

"I'd like you to dress nicely for lunch," Kate said. "Suits and ties for the gentlemen."

At around eleven o'clock *Ciao* began to turn, and Gloria went forward to find out why.

"This is as close as I want to get to Havana," the captain said, pulling the power back. "*Trafalgar III* is only about half an hour out of Havana now."

"Where are we going?"

"To Key West — that's all there is. We have enough fuel at our normal cruising speed of ten knots."

"When will we get in?"

"After dark."

Everybody went below to change clothes, and when they came up, Stone pointed. "Morro Castle," he said. "I've seen pictures. We're about to be in Havana Harbor."

"I know," Holly said.

"You're in on this?"

"I follow my leader."

"Why are we here?"

"Official business," Holly replied.

They slowed as they approached the harbor limits, and Kate addressed them.

"Thank you for being such good sports and not asking questions," she said. "We will shortly be taking aboard the president of Cuba and his party."

# 49

The Cuban party were traveling aboard a naval patrol boat, dressed with all her signal flags for the occasion. Stone looked up and saw that *Trafalgar III* had dressed ship, as well.

The launch drew alongside in the approaches to Havana Harbor, and the two crews made her fast, and *Trafalgar III* lowered her boarding ladder. Two Cuban naval officers were first aboard, then two policeman-looking types, then a pair of gentlemen in suits and ties, followed by the Cuban president.

The two presidents shook hands and exchanged warm greetings, then Kate introduced her party, and the *presidente* his. She escorted him to the dining table, where two stacks of documents and pens were laid out. The two presidents sat down and, at Holly's instructions, each began signing a stack, then they exchanged stacks and started again, while Secret Service agents photo-graphed and videotaped their progress. When they were done, the two of them met on one side of the table, and Kate escorted everyone into the saloon, where champagne was being poured.

"What just happened?" Stone whispered to Holly.

"The United States' embargo on Cuba has been lifted, and the two countries now have full and normal diplomatic relations. One of the Cuban suits is the new ambas-sador to the United States. Kate is still in the process of appointing ours to them."

They returned to the dining room, where the table had been set for lunch, and for the next hour there was cheerful conversation among the lunchers, while the photogra-phers covered everyone.

At the appointed hour, the *presidente* and his party rose, said their farewells, and car-rying a briefcase full of signed documents, returned to their naval vessel and were cast off.

*Trafalgar III*'s engines were started, her anchor weighed, and the yacht left Havana Harbor and turned to the north.

Half an hour later her passengers were scattered around the yacht in their usual cruise wear — swimsuits or shorts.

An hour after that a United States Navy destroyer hove into view, and the two ships lay, dead in the water, thirty yards apart, while a Secret Service launch delivered a package to the destroyer, then the two vessels got under way again, and the destroyer resumed its station just over the horizon.

"What was that all about?" Stone asked Holly.

"They were delivering the photographs and videos to the Navy, who will upload them to a satellite, which will beam them down to the Pentagon and the White House, which will release the story to the media and the press."

"It's all terribly efficient, isn't it?"

*Ciao* reached Key West just after dark and put into the Galleon Marina, on the outside line of berths, near the main channel into the harbor. On the passage back, Gloria had written a piece called "Mystery Yacht," which she e-mailed back to Hazel at *Just Folks*.

She and Bobby Marks were having a before-dinner cocktail when their captain came into the saloon. "*Trafalgar III* is passing in the channel just now," he said.

They went into the aft cockpit to watch her pass and turn into the Coast Guard docks, followed closely by *Scout.*

Judy, the cook, came up from below. "Turn on the television," she said.

They went back into the saloon, and the captain switched on the satellite TV. A banner, "BREAKING NEWS," filled the screen, and an anchorwoman was reading from a sheet of paper in her hand. "This afternoon, aboard a British vessel in Havana Harbor, the American and Cuban presidents signed an agreement establishing full diplomatic relations between the two countries, and, more importantly, ending the United States' embargo on trade with Cuba. From noon on January first, there will be free and open trade between the two countries, and American citizens will be able to travel to Cuba without a visa, requiring only an American passport for entry into Cuba and for returning to the USA. Today's act ends more than seventy years of official enmity between the two countries."

"Jesus Christ!" Gloria said. "We've been had! At least we have those photographs." Her telephone rang.

"Hello?"

"Gloria? It's Hazel. I got your stuff, and it's a sweet story, but we can't publish nude photographs of the President of the United States and the secretary of state."

*"What?"*

"Why are you shocked? That doesn't fit with our new, more sophisticated format, and anyway, the secretary is in the company of one of our owners, Stone Barrington. Remember him?"

"Are you telling me those naked people on Loggerhead Key were the Presidents Lee?"

"I am. Surely you knew that."

"I didn't know it until this minute. Have you been watching TV for the past few minutes?"

"No."

"Well, in the middle of last night, *Trafalgar III* weighed anchor and headed south. We followed as soon as we could, but we didn't have the paperwork for Cuba, nor the fuel to go all the way."

"She went to Havana?"

"Yes, and President Lee and the Cuban president signed a document ending the Cuban embargo and establishing full diplomatic relations."

"Holy shit! And you missed that story?"

"Hazel, the entire world missed that story. I told you, we didn't have fuel or the documents to follow. *Trafalgar III* is docking next door at the Coast Guard facility as we speak, and we can't get in there to interview anybody."

"So we're completely shut out?"

"No more than anybody else. Hang on a minute." She covered the phone. "Bobby, grab your camera bag and find a spot from where you can shoot the Coast Guard docks. Shimmy up somebody's mast, if you have to!"

"Hazel, we're going to try to get photographs of the yacht and anybody aboard it that we can see. I'll call you back." She hung up.

"For Christ's sake, Bobby, hurry!"

Half an hour later, the Lees' luggage was taken off the yacht, and the other passengers walked them ashore and to their waiting car to say their goodbyes, while the crew peeled the borrowed name off the stern and replaced the White Ensign with an American yacht ensign.

"It was absolutely wonderful, Stone, every minute of it," Kate said, hugging him. They got into their car and were driven away, and the other passengers returned to the yacht for dinner.

Bobby Marks came, panting, back aboard *Ciao.* "I got them, Gloria," he said, grinning. "All of them, and with my long lens it looks like we're standing next to them. The light was good, too, from the docks' flood lamps, and the yacht's real name is *Breeze.*"

Gloria got on the phone to Hazel. "Sweetheart," she said, "check your e-mail — we got more of the story than anybody, and I'm rewriting the rest!"

The Gulfstream jet set down smoothly at Warm Springs and taxied to the ramp, where a three-car motorcade awaited them. There was no press or media present, since they had not been informed.

The motorcade proceeded quietly through the warm Georgia night to the Lee farm, where they were greeted by Aunt Beatrice. "Billy's sound asleep in his room," she said. "Why don't you look in on him?"

Kate and Will tiptoed into Will's childhood room, now Billy's, and regarded the sleeping child with parental affection.

The following day, with press and media present, the Lee family boarded the Gulfstream and flew back to Andrews Air Force Base, near Washington, from where they were choppered back to the White House.

The daily White House press briefing that morning was bedlam.

# 50

The following morning after their cruise, Stone and his party took off from Key West International, and he dropped Holly and the Rules at Manassas two hours later. Holly gave Stone a big kiss. "I'll see you New Year's Eve," she said, "if the world can keep it together until then." After a pause to take on additional fuel, Stone took off and flew to Teterboro, where Fred and Bob awaited him and the Bacchettis in the Bentley. He dropped Dino and Viv off at home, then continued to his own.

Joan greeted him in the office. "Thank you so much for the *beautiful* cashmere sweater, and the staff thanks you for their gifts and their bonuses."

"You're all very welcome," Stone said. He regarded the dog. "Has Bob gained weight?"

"Ah, um . . . Well, it was Christmas, wasn't it? He got an extra cookie or two."

"You're a complete patsy," Stone replied.

"Where that dog is concerned, you're absolutely right," Joan said. "Did you see the President on TV in Havana?"

"Joan, I was there. The ceremony took place aboard *Breeze.*"

"Oh, I had no idea!"

"Neither did I, and I hope no one else catches on. I don't want another deluge of press calls. We woke up that morning on the way to Cuba. I didn't know where I was until I saw Morro Castle."

"That must have been some meeting!"

"A good time was had by all. We were back in Key West in time for dinner."

Gloria got in later that day. A message was on her phone from Alphonse Teppi, and she called him back.

"Listen, sweetheart," Al said, "I was on Barrington like a clam, but Danny lost him that same day and we never found him again."

"I found him," Gloria replied.

"Oh? Where?"

"About sixty miles west of Key West."

"Florida?"

"There's only one."

"I read the President was down there somewhere, too."

318

"They were on the same yacht, which left us in the dust, so to speak, then went to Cuba. We managed to photograph them when they were back in Key West."

"Holy shit!"

"Exactly."

"Danny wants to know if you want him to kill Barrington."

"Yeah, sure, tell him to get right on it." The only worse numskull than Al, she reflected, was Danny. She hung up and called Hazel.

"You're back!"

"I am. How did you like the shots in Key West?"

"They were perfect, and we're the only ones who have them. When we publish tomorrow, the *Times* and the networks will be *extremely* jealous. I especially liked the shots of them ripping off the name and exposing the real one."

"I certainly hope so," Gloria said. "Bobby risked his neck to get those shots from the top of a utility pole!" She hung up, and the phone rang immediately.

"Hello?"

"It's Benton. Welcome home."

"Hey, baby."

"Chinese at your place tonight?"

"I'd rather go out to dinner," she said.

"Someplace splashy, where everybody will see us together."

He laughed. "All right, why not? You're on. I'll pick you up at seven-thirty."

"See you then, babe." She hung up, gratified.

Dino called.

"Yeah?"

"Patroon, seven-thirty? Just you and me, Viv's flown the coop again."

"You betcha. See ya then." Stone hung up.

Stone and Dino were still on their first drink at Patroon when Benton Blake and Gloria Parsons walked in together. They didn't see Stone across the room until they had sat down.

Stone raised a glass to them, then sent them a bottle of Veuve Clicquot La Grande Dame. They looked pleased.

A moment later, a waiter brought over a magazine on a silver tray. "It's *Just Folks,*" Stone said, examining the cover. "Tomorrow's edition." He was astonished that it was a beautiful photograph of *Breeze,* probably taken last summer.

"Nice shot of the yacht," Dino remarked.

"Yes, it is," Stone replied, "but why?" He

looked at a Post-it stuck to the cover. *See pages 16–20. G.*

He opened the magazine to find a double-page spread of a photograph of Kate and Will's departure from the yacht. It had been taken from a height and was very clear.

"Looks like she had a drone," Dino said.

Stone flipped through the piece, which ended with a shot of him and Holly jumping from the yacht the first morning, with suitably blanked-out parts. "Looks like we were under surveillance the whole time," Stone said.

"But not in Cuba — no shots from there."

"No, no shots from there. They got one of the yacht's name being changed, though." It was written under the pseudonym Laurentia Scott-Peebles. He scanned the piece quickly. She seemed to know everything they had done on their cruise, including the voyage to Cuba. She had to have been aboard the smaller yacht *Ciao,* but it almost sounded as if she'd been aboard *Breeze.*

"Well," Dino said, "you got away with it until tomorrow."

## 51

Alphonse Teppi and Danny Blaine took a table at a place on the West Side, near Danny's office. Shortly, a friend of Danny's joined them.

"Al," Danny said, "this is Crank Jackson. We went to graduate school together."

"Oh?" Al asked. "Where?"

"Fishkill."

Crank Jackson was short, with a shaved head, but he managed to be imposing. Al spotted part of a prison-style tattoo on his neck, under his shirt collar. "What did you guys study?" Al asked, smirking.

"I majored in science — breaking limbs," Crank replied, returning the smirk. "Danny studied the fine arts — pickpocketing."

"I got pretty good at it, too."

"Where's the can?" Crank asked.

"Over there, behind the cash register," Al replied, and watched Crank pick his way through the tables with considerable grace of movement.

"Crank is your general all-round criminal," Danny said, "he just specializes in leg-breaking — he used to work for a shylock who didn't like people who missed payments."

"Yeah? What's he doing these days?"

"Whatever he's asked to do — you name it. For five grand, his standard fee, Crank will remove a person's head from his torso, or anything else you'd like done."

"Well, then," Al said, "Crank could come in very useful."

"How so?"

"I spoke to Gloria, she's back from her trip, and she's still mad at Barrington. She'd like him to have a serious accident — fatal."

"Great!" Danny replied with enthusiasm. "I'm so sick of following the guy I'd be glad to see him go."

"Up to you how, pal," Al said.

"You think she means it?"

"Yes, and sooner rather than later."

They saw Crank returning from the men's room.

"The means are at hand," Danny said, "and we don't have to get our hands dirty."

Crank fell back into his chair. "What are you guys looking so smug about?"

"We were just talking about you, Crank,"

Danny said. "And what you do so well."

Crank grinned. "Lay it on me."

Joan came into Stone's office the following morning. "It seems you have won the favor of the media again," she said.

"Oh, no."

"I have five requests for a TV interview — including Charlie Rose and the *Today* show. I told the other three, politely, to get lost."

"Well, you can tell the *Today* show, politely, and Charlie, *very* politely, that my lips are sealed on the subject of the cruise, and I do not confirm nor deny anything, including whether I have an interest in *Breeze,* which is owned by a Delaware corporation, if they try to trace her."

"Gotcha, boss. Same with the print people?"

"Nothing to say, and I decline to say it."

"It only makes you more interesting to them, you know."

"Remember what happened when you advised me to talk to one of them, and the others would go away?"

"I seem to recall that," she replied. "It didn't end well, did it?"

"Well, it finally seems to have been straightened out, or at least it seemed so until *that* came out." He pointed at the copy of *Just Folks* on his desk.

"I've already read it," Joan said. "Oops, your phone." She picked up the one on his desk. "The Barrington Group at Woodman & Weld," she said, then listened and covered the phone. "Will you speak to the President of the United States?" she asked archly.

Stone took the phone from her. "This is Stone Barrington."

"Just one moment, Mr. Barrington," the operator said.

There was a click, then: "Good morning, Stone," Kate Lee said.

He was relieved that she sounded cheerful.

"Well, I guess we couldn't keep it a secret forever, but at least we weren't found out until it was over."

"I've no idea how they caught on," Stone said.

"I do. Word got around Key West that some British dignitary was aboard — maybe the prime minister or a rock star. I don't think they knew I was there until I was back in Georgia for the night."

"How's Billy?"

"He loved seeing his pony. He wants me to build a stable on the White House lawn."

"The Republicans in Congress would just love that."

"Wouldn't they? I just wanted you to know that, with your help, we accomplished our purpose, and I'm not in the least sorry that they found us out when it was over."

"Thank you, Kate."

She wished him a happy new year and hung up.

Joan Buzzed him. "The secretary of state on line one."

He picked up. "Good morning."

"Same to you. I'm getting into a chopper now, I'll be there in time for lunch."

"Want me to meet you at the heliport?"

"Nope. The State Department doesn't regard you as having any security benefit attached. The guys with the guns will deposit me on your doorstep, then flee."

"See you then." Stone hung up and buzzed Joan.

"Yessir?"

"Ask Helene to whip up something for lunch for Holly and me."

"Sure thing."


Danny Blaine and Crank Jackson were riding uptown in an Uber. They got out on Stone's corner. "Tell me, Crank," Danny said, "where'd you get your nickname?"

"From a prison guard," Crank replied. "He liked my action when I broke a guy's neck in the yard, once."

"Ah. Okay, we're going to walk quickly down the south side of the street. When I tell you to, take a good look at the house on your left, the one with the garage door, but don't slow down. We don't want to be noticed by anyone inside."

"Gotcha," Crank replied.

They walked down the block, and Crank swiveled his head left for a long moment. "Got it," he said.

"The guy works at home but goes out for lunch occasionally, sometimes in a Bentley that looks armored, so it's no good shooting him through a window. Sometimes he walks to a restaurant though."

"I need a motorcycle," Crank said.

"Steal one."

"Can do. I need a .22 with a silencer. We don't want to have the whole neighborhood calling nine-one-one at the same time."

"It's a straight five grand, Crank." Danny handed him an envelope. "Here's a grand, the rest on delivery. Anything you need comes out of your end."

"Fair enough."

# 52

Crank visited a pawnshop on the Lower East Side and selected a .22 semiautomatic pistol and a nicely crafted silencer from the owner's private stock in the cellar. He was allowed to test fire it once for noise. It made a *plip* sound. "Very nice," he replied, and negotiated the price from a thousand down to seven hundred.

"I'll buy it back for two hundred when you're done," his supplier said. "I can change the ballistics."

"I need a set of bolt cutters, too," Crank said.

"The hardware store is three doors down, on your right."

Crank stuffed the pistol into the inside pocket of his parka and the silencer in another, then visited the hardware store and bought a short-handled bolt cutter and a screwdriver.

The motorcycle theft took a little longer:

he wanted something on the light side, but with enough power to speed through traffic, and conventionally muffled. No Harley noise for this job. He found a nice little Honda, conveniently stuffed between two parked cars, which hid his actions. He removed the license plate and exchanged it for one on another cycle down the block, then he went back to the Honda, cut the chain anchoring it to a street sign, and did a little magic to get it started. The helmet on board was, not surprisingly, too small, so he put up the hood on his parka. Shortly, he was on his way uptown for a little more reconnoitering.

He pulled up a few doors up the street from the Barrington house and watched as a heavy-duty SUV, followed by another, stopped and disgorged a woman and a couple of suitcases. She went to a door bearing a brass plate, rang a bell, and was met by another woman, who held the door while she and her luggage were put inside.

The woman who opened the door saw him up the street and took a good long look at him before closing the door behind her.

Crank didn't like that; it made him feel amateurish. He decided not to attract further attention by roaring away. Instead, he took a *New York Post* from his parka pocket and pretended to read it. A couple of minutes later, the suspicious woman opened the door again and looked up and down the block. This time she *glared* at him before going inside again.

Crank put away his paper, started the bike, and motored gently away. He caught her in his rearview mirror as she came outside again, this time holding a hand slightly behind her. The bitch was carrying! He'd have to watch out for her.

"I heard from Kate this morning," Stone said to Holly, after he had poured them a drink and sat her down.

"How did she sound?"

"Cheerful. I was afraid she'd be annoyed that we made the papers."

"Annoyed? What would she have to be annoyed about? We got away clean."

"Well, after the fact, anyway."

"Do you know what would have happened if the media had got wind of our little cruise? We'd have had a flotilla of boats, bristling with all sorts of cameras, sailing just as close to us as the Coast Guard and the Navy would have allowed. *That* would have annoyed her."

"And you, too," Stone said, laughing. "As it was, you got photographed naked. It's lucky I have an interest in that magazine."

"I remind you, *you* were also naked at the time, and I wouldn't be too surprised if that photograph didn't get pirated out to other, less scrupulous publications that you don't own."

"You mean . . ."

"Yes, you'll be waving in the wind, for all the world to see."

"And all the world would know that you had gone Brazilian."

Holly roared. "Just imagine, I'd never live that down."

"Probably not. You could never run for office."

Holly looked startled. "Where did you hear that?"

"Hear what?"

"That I might run for office."

"I've never heard that at any time. What office did you have in mind?"

"I didn't have *any* office in mind," she replied.

"But somebody brought it up?"

She looked away.

"Kate?"

"Maybe."

"What office?"

Holly held up a hand. "Stop, you're embarrassing me."

"You're not easily embarrassed — what's going on?"

"Nothing is going on, she just brought it up the last time we were in the Oval together."

"And when was that?"

"This morning."

"Wait a minute — do you mean . . ."

"I haven't said a word — you remember that."

"What, exactly, did Kate say?"

"Well, she mentioned that my four years as national security advisor had gone very well, and they went down well with Congress, too. After all, I did sail through the Senate Foreign Relations Committee hearing, when she nominated me."

"That is so. As I recall, the vote was unanimous, and when your nomination came to the floor, only one senator voted against you."

"Oh, that was Flora Ridges, the idiot from Oklahoma. She votes against anything that comes from Kate."

"So, Kate thinks you might have a shot at the Big One?"

Holly actually blushed. "Don't you ever say that to another person."

Stone thought about it for a moment. "I think Kate is right."

"Now, don't *you* start."

"There's no one in the party out front to succeed Kate," Stone pointed out.

"True enough, but they'll start coming out of the woodwork pretty soon," Holly said.

"There's nobody out there you couldn't take. What is Kate's plan?"

"How do you know she has a plan?"

"Kate always has a plan."

"Well, I'm addressing the UN in her place next week, so you'll have me on your hands a little longer."

"Fine with me." He thought a little more. "I suppose I'm going to have to drop out of the picture."

"Kate thinks your presence in my life is already baked in, that it won't matter if the world knows I'm fucking somebody. She thinks it might even help." She smoothed her skirt. "It also helps if the world knows I'm not fucking *everybody.*"

"What else does Kate have planned?"

"I'm going to be present at more of her events and speeches, especially in the swing states."

"Good idea. I think you should do more serious interviews, too."

"I'm doing *Meet the Press* next Sunday. Word is, Chuck Todd thinks I'm hot."

"Lots of people think you're hot."

"I'm lucky Katty Kay is British."

Stone raised his glass. "Today *Meet the Press* — tomorrow, the world!"

# 53

Gloria unpacked two very large bags at Benton Blake's uptown apartment, then checked her makeup and went into the living room, where Blake poured them a drink.

"All settled in?" he asked.

"For the moment," she said, accepting the martini.

"It's best that you don't spend every night here just yet. Give the press people a chance to see us together a few times. Then, when we're no longer such an item, you can move in and get rid of your apartment."

"I like the sound of that," she said. "Listen . . ."

"I'm listening."

"Do we really need to go to the Bacchettis' tonight?"

"Do you have something against the Bacchettis?"

"No, I like them, but Stone Barrington will certainly be there."

"You're going to have to get used to seeing Stone. He's my law partner, after all, and he was very cordial last night, sending us the champagne. A very good champagne, too."

"I'm still nervous around him."

"He won't bite. He clearly wants to make peace, so don't resist it."

"Who will be at the Bacchettis'?"

"A few cops and judges, a few minor celebrities, the mayor, certainly. God knows who else. They have a wide acquaintance and a big apartment."

Her cell rang. She glanced at it in her handbag: Danny. She sent it to voice mail. Danny was a part of her earlier life that she wanted to put behind her.

"Anything important?"

"Far less than important," she replied. The phone rang again: Al. She sent it to voice mail.

"Still unimportant?" Benton asked.

"It's time I put away childish things," she said, "and childish people."

"Everybody has baggage," he replied.

Stone and Holly were still having their talk when Joan buzzed, and Stone picked up the study phone. "Yes?"

"There was a thug on a motorcycle eyeballing the house a few minutes ago," she said.

"Did you shoot him dead?" She had done that before.

"Not yet, but I'd better not see him again, I don't like thugs on motorcycles."

"Well, I'm not crazy about bodies in the street, so contain yourself."

"I'll try."

Stone hung up. "Joan saw somebody she didn't like on the street, and she's thinking of shooting him."

"Does she do that often?"

"Rarely, but she thinks about it a lot. I think the .45 in her desk drawer makes her feel powerful."

"The Secret Service could use her — maybe I can get her a new job."

"If you took away Joan, I'd have to shoot myself. I don't know how to do anything without her."

"I know that. I was just trying to frighten you with my influence."

"At some point," he said, "we're going to have to talk about what happens to us when you run, and even worse, after you're elected."

"Let's jump off that bridge when we come to it," she said.

"All right. Would you like to hear about

our plans for the evening?"

"You don't want to surprise me?"

"You hate surprises."

"That's true. All right, tell me about it."

"We're going to see Michael Feinstein's holiday show, the eight-o'clock performance, at Studio 54, then we're going to Dino and Viv's New Year's Eve party in plenty of time for midnight."

"That all sounds perfectly delightful — you should have surprised me."

"I miss Bobby Short at the Café Carlyle, but he up and died on me. He and Elaine."

"Everybody does that — it's catching."

"Still, Michael Feinstein is a worthy successor, and I have a shot at outliving him."

"Speaking of living, what sort of shape are you in?"

"You have to ask?"

"Not that — heart, lungs, liver, especially liver."

"I had my FAA physical a while back. The doctor said everything was, and I quote, 'perfectly normal.' "

"I'm glad to hear it."

"What about you? Will you live into a second term?"

"Well, I saw my gynecologist last week — did you know we have a staff gynecologist at the White House now?"

"I did not know that. I expect it was Kate's idea."

"It was my idea, actually, but Kate bought it. After all, we have a lot of women on the White House staff."

"And what did he have to say?"

"*She* said I'm not getting enough sex, but apart from that, I'm startlingly healthy."

"I'll do everything I can to help."

"You're doing just fine," she said. "If you were living in Washington, I'd have a hard time getting up in the mornings."

"That's the nicest thing anybody's said to me in this millennium," Stone replied.

"And the truest," she replied. "You can let it go to your head, if you want to."

Crank Jackson parked between two cars around the corner and made a couple of passes up and down the block. This time he turned his reversible parka inside out and put a folding tweed hat on his bald head.

Joan saw him pass outside her window, but she fell for the disguise and did not connect him with the previous thug. She did notice when he returned up the block, but then he disappeared around the corner.

Crank returned to his motorcycle and found

a parking ticket taped to the handlebars. He stuffed it into a pocket. The switched license plates would put the wrong bike in the wrong place, if it ever came to that. He would switch plates again later, if he had the opportunity.

He checked his watch: seven o'clock, too early for Barrington to be going out on the town on New Year's Eve. He got back on the motorcycle and looked for a place to have a quick bite; he'd be back on station by seven-thirty.

# 54

Stone tied his bow tie in one sweeping, nonstop motion. Perfect. He'd seen Cary Grant do that in a movie once, and he practiced it for years before he finally could do it.

"I saw that," Holly said from over his shoulder, "and I'm very impressed."

"Nothing to it; it just comes naturally, I guess."

She was dressed in his favorite color on her, an emerald-green dress that worked so well with her auburn hair. "Wow," he said.

"You always say that."

He shrugged. "You always wow me. The White House press is going to love you."

"They don't love anybody for very long."

"They love Kate."

"If they did, would she have to pull off an elaborate ruse in order to have an undisturbed vacation?"

"You have a point."

"And by their attitude, they screwed themselves out of the diplomatic story of the year, which she pulled off without a hitch because they weren't looking over her shoulder."

"They sort of shot themselves in the foot, didn't they?"

"They do that all the time, without seeming to notice."

"What's the old saying? Insanity is doing the same thing over and over while expecting a different outcome?"

"That's sort of the old saying. I can't remember it exactly but your version will do. Yes, they do that."

"Are you hungry?"

"Starved."

"Well, dinner is part of the New Year's thing at the Feinstein show, but we have to eat again at Dino and Viv's or they'll be hurt, so go easy on the first dinner."

"I've never gone easy on a dinner in my life," she said. "I have the kind of metabolism that burns up food faster than I can eat it."

"Is that why I've never noticed your gaining a pound?"

"I've never gained a pound," she explained. "Don't ever repeat that to a woman, she'll hate me forever."

"So the big secret, when you're in the White House, is . . ."

"That I eat like a horse and never gain weight. If you ever tell *anybody,* I'll have you deported."

"Speaking of getting deported, how do I get you to my place in England without the country collapsing in your absence?"

"There's going to be a big confab with European leaders in April, in London. Maybe I can vanish for a few days, like Kate."

"I'll have to work on a plan," Stone said, "with diversions and everything."

"Run it by me so I can build it into my schedule. It's not too early to start planning."


Crank Jackson was a little late getting back to Turtle Bay, and as he turned the corner he saw the green Bentley emerge from the Barrington garage, just in time for him to follow. It surprised him how difficult it was for a motorcycle to follow a car in midtown Manhattan on New Year's Eve. Traffic kept coming to a halt, blocking the gaps, and he would have to pull over to the curb to wait for a light to change. Very annoying. He would have to transfer the anger into a fund reserved for killing Stone Barrington.

The car eventually made it to West Fifty-fourth Street, near Eighth Avenue, and Barrington and his girlfriend got out of the car and stepped into the crowd rushing the door. No opportunity. Then the car drove away and, to his further annoyance, went back to Turtle Bay and into the garage. The driver was obviously not going to wait outside for Barrington to emerge.

Crank decided his mark was having dinner and seeing a show, so he decided to find a place for dessert and come back in, say, an hour and a half.

The show was terrific: all the music Stone loved best, and Holly enjoyed herself, too. Stone ate a third of his dinner and had his plate taken away before he could weaken, but Holly ate everything. She had apparently not been kidding about her capacity.

Somewhat to his surprise, Stone spotted Alphonse Teppi across the room with a woman. He hadn't expected that. Teppi saw him, too, and pretended to ignore him.

When he got a chance, Teppi called Danny Blaine.

"Yeah?"

"Where are you?"

"At a *W* party, downtown."

"Is your guy on the job tonight?"

"He is."

"Tell him his target is at Studio 54 and will be until the show is over around ten o'clock."

"Right." He hung up.

Danny called Crank.

"Yeah?"

"Where are you?"

"At a restaurant on Second Avenue, having dessert."

"Good. Your guy is at Studio 54 until around ten."

"I know, I followed him there and suspected he'd be awhile."

"Don't lose him, this needs to be done tonight."

"Why?"

"Don't ask questions, just earn your money."

"Gotcha."

Crank was back in Turtle Bay by 9:30 and watched as the Bentley left the garage. More traffic, more stops. Finally, in a bust of glee, Crank gunned the Honda and zipped uptown between lanes of traffic. After all, he knew where the car was going, and he was there, waiting, when the Bentley pulled up to the line of limos in front of the door. Eventually, Barrington and the woman came outside and found the car, then Crank was in for another round of stop-and-go traffic.

They went up Madison Avenue and took a right on East Sixty-third Street, and looking down the block, Crank thought he had come upon the policeman's ball. He counted four police cars and SUVs double-parked, two of them with lights flashing, and at least a dozen cops outside the building on the corner, standing around and waiting for something terrible to happen.

Crank made his way down the street slowly, legs out, skimming the ground, and because of the clot of traffic he was able to get a really good look at what was going on. He reckoned everyone would pour into the place and then start trickling out after the midnight toast.

"What the hell," he said aloud to himself, "I may as well take in a movie and catch 'em coming out."

# 55

Stone and Holly had to wait until two elevator loads had gone upstairs before them. Finally, they stepped into the vestibule of the Bacchetti apartment, where a helper was taking coats. Stone was glad they had left theirs in the car, and Holly wore a stole over her shoulders.

They worked their way across the living room, shaking a hand here and there. Stone noticed he got a lot more attention because Holly was his date; most of them had never met a secretary of state.

They finally reached Dino and Viv and embraced both.

"Wow," Dino commented on Holly's dress.

"You never gain a pound, do you?" Viv asked.

"I have to watch my weight like a hawk," Holly replied with a groan for emphasis.

Shortly, Benton Blake and Gloria Parsons entered the room, and the former governor was rushed by nearly everybody there. Gloria clung to his arm, to keep the crowd from coming between them. And then they were face-to-face with Stone Barrington and Holly Barker.

Gloria shrank from them, but Benton pushed her forward and Stone introduced them both to Holly. Gloria wondered if one curtsied to a secretary of state.

"Loved your piece in that magazine," Holly said, without a trace of a smile.

"Sorry," Gloria said, "it's the nature of the beast."

"Stone loved it, too," Holly said, rubbing it in. "It did wonders for his reputation."

"Which is well earned," Benton said, stepping in to rescue her. He and Stone shook hands warmly. Fortunately, a waiter appeared with champagne, which gave the ex-governor an opportunity to change the subject. "I haven't seen you around the office," he said to Stone.

"I come in a couple of times a week, if there's a meeting I can't handle on the computer," Stone replied. "I like working at home."

"All alone?" Benton asked.

"The company is good."

Everybody laughed, easing the tension.

A man in a tuxedo that was a little too tight for him approached and shook Stone's hand.

"Have you met Holly Barker, Chief?" Stone asked. "Holly, this is Deputy Chief Mallory."

"How do you do, Madam Secretary? I'll be supervising your security detail for your UN speech this week."

"Thank you for your concern, Chief," Holly replied. "Tell me, how many officers will the department be wasting on that detail? Nobody is interested in killing me."

"A couple of dozen officers will have that privilege, but I assure you, they will not be wasted. We would not want anything untoward to happen to such a charming lady."

"I'm overwhelmed," Holly said, smiling, trying to set the man at ease. Someone tugged at his sleeve and he wandered gratefully off into the next room.

Holly tugged at Stone's sleeve. "I'm hungry," she said.

"Well, that wasn't as bad as it could have been," Gloria said, "though she did find a way to tell me off without yelling."

"People in your business should have to meet their quarry face-to-face more often,"

Benton said. "It would be character-building."

"You think my character needs building?" she asked.

"More character, less journalist could be a good idea."

"I'll keep that in mind."

Crank Jackson got out of his movie at half past eleven and found another parking ticket on his motorcycle. This one will be good, he thought; it will place me more than a mile from the scene of the crime. He got it started and drove back to East Sixty-third Street. Traffic was much improved; he drove slowly past the building and saw that the cops were now mostly in the lobby, keeping warm. He drove around the block once more and noticed that there was only one police car parked out front, now, and the driver was apparently inside with the rest of his colleagues.

Crank turned downtown on Park Avenue and backed the cycle between two limos, whose drivers had sought warmth and companionship somewhere else. Now he was only a few yards from the building's entrance, around the corner, and Park Avenue would be a good escape route downtown when he had to run for it.

He checked his watch: a quarter to twelve. Then, as he watched, Barrington's green Bentley came around the corner and doubled-parked on the avenue, one car down from where Crank had settled in. Now Barrington and his lady would have to come to him, making his work much easier and his escape surer.

# 56

Everybody counted backward from ten while watching the big ball on TV fall in Times Square, then they sang "Auld Lang Syne," even if nobody understood the words.

"Whew!" Stone said. "We made it through another one. You ready to go home?"

"I just want to have a look at dessert," Holly said, leading him through the waning crowd toward the groaning board. "You want some?"

"Maybe half a slice of mince pie," Stone said, following her.

"The bread pudding looks wonderful," Holly said, adding some caramel sauce and a scoop of ice cream to hers. She took a big bite of everything. "It *is* wonderful!"

Stone returned most of his pie to a passing waiter, then went into Dino's study and collapsed into a comfortable leather chair. The mayor was sitting opposite him.

"Happy new year, Barrington," the man said. He tended to use last names only when speaking to men: fewer names to remember.

"Yer Honor, the same to you," Stone replied. "How've you been?"

"Tolerable, I guess you could say. I'm trying to sober up enough to get myself out of this armchair."

"Don't fight it," Stone said, "just sit back and enjoy. Can I get you another drink?" While hizzoner was thinking about that, Stone flagged down a waiter and snagged two loaded brandy snifters, handing one to the mayor.

"Better times," Stone said, raising his glass.

"I'll sure as hell drink to that," the mayor replied.

"Tell me, which is more fun — police commissioner or mayor?" The man had held both jobs.

"*Fun?*" the man exploded. "I don't think I've had a day's fun in either one. They're both like a slog through deep snow — or more likely, deep shit."

"What was your worst day?"

"Every single police funeral I attended," he replied, "and I attended them all, as commissioner or mayor, most of them shootings, but if somebody's dog bit him on the ankle and he fell down the stairs, I attended that, too."

"A sad duty. I've attended a few, myself."

"I hear you were a much better detective than anybody gave you credit for," the mayor said.

"Those are kind words, sir."

"Ever wish you'd stuck with it?"

"I didn't have that opportunity. They elbowed me out at the first opportunity."

"I remember that," the mayor said. "I was chief of detectives at the time, but they had that medical report, and there was nothing I could do."

"Well, I guess I landed on my feet," Stone said. "I've no complaints."

"I should think not!" the mayor snorted.

Holly appeared. "Okay, I'm stuffed. We can go."

"Mr. Mayor, may I introduce the secretary of state, Holly Barker? Madam Secretary, His Honor, the mayor of New York City."

"We met a long time ago," she said, "when you were a deputy chief of police and I was running the CIA station in the city."

"Ah, yes," the mayor said. "I remember when it blew up."

"There was that," Holly replied ruefully.

"That was the nastiest explosion we've ever had in this town," he said. "I'm glad you weren't hurt. Tell me, Madam Secretary, have you ever considered running for President?"

Holly put the back of a hand to her forehead and feigned a swoon. "God forbid," she said.

"You keep thinking about it," the mayor said. "I'll announce my support the first day, for what that's worth."

"It would be worth a great deal," Holly said, "and if the day should ever dawn, I'll come looking for you."

Stone, sensing she was uncomfortable, rose and made leaving noises. They said good night to the mayor and to their hosts and lined up for the elevator again.

Gloria Parsons made her way to the powder room, locked herself in, set her bag down by the loo, pulled everything down, and sat. As she did, she spotted her cell phone in her bag, which she had neglected for some days. There were two phone messages, and she pressed the button. The first was from Al Teppi, and she listened in horror. "That stupid shit! Doesn't he know from sarcasm?"

Someone knocked on the door. "Anyone in there?"

"Occupied!" Glora yelled, pressing the

other button. It was Danny. He and Al were both insane, and Danny was asking for another four thousand dollars. *Another* four thousand? She threw the phone at the bag, pulled up her thong, and wrestled with the door lock, finally getting it open and startling the woman waiting outside.

She ran into the living room, looking around, then spotted Stone Barrington and Holly Barker getting onto the elevator. She yelled his name as the doors closed and the dozen people waiting for the next ride all turned and looked at her.

Benton Blake appeared at her side. "What's going on?" he asked.

She grabbed his hand and towed him toward the stairs. "Come on!" she hissed.

"What's going on?"

"I've got to stop them," she said.

"Stop who?"

She slammed the fire door behind her, took off her heels, and bolted down the stairs, with Benton in pursuit.

"Gloria, what the hell?"

"Shut up and follow me!" she shouted, and kept running.

Crank Jackson loitered behind a large mailbox, which gave him good cover, and watched the door of the apartment building. He took the pistol from his inside pocket and the silencer from his outer pocket and began screwing one into the other. Finally he worked the action, feeding a round into the chamber, and flicked off the safety.

Stone and Holly filed out of the elevator with the others, and as they entered the lobby, a blast of cold air blew in.

"It's going to be freezing out there," Holly said.

"Don't worry, I spoke to Fred, and he's parked just around the corner to the right with the heat on, so you won't be cold for long."

Fred got out of the car, dressed only in his suit, and shivered in the night air, watching the corner for his passengers' approach. As he did he saw a man in a black coat with a hood standing behind a mailbox, staring at the building with interest, with something long and black in his hand.

Gloria burst through the downstairs door and into the lobby, her bare feet freezing on the cold marble floor. "Stone!" she yelled, as he disappeared out the front door. She began fighting her way through the crowd of revelers and cops in the lobby.

■ ■ ■ ■

Crank Jackson spotted them coming and raised the pistol, resting it on top of the mailbox. He sighted on Barrington's forehead and waited for him to reach the corner of the building. As he did, he began squeezing the trigger very slowly.

Stone took Holly's hand and pulled her across his body to the right, to give her some shelter from the side of the building. As he did, he heard two noises almost simultaneously: one, a *plip,* the other, a very loud bang.

# 57

Holly flinched, took a step back, and said, "Ow, goddamnit!"

"Did you break a heel?" Stone asked, looking down at the sidewalk for the object in question.

"No," Holly said angrily, "I've been shot, and I'm getting blood on this fucking dress."

Stone turned her around and surveyed her; there was blood soaking through her gauzy stole.

"Mr. Barrington!" It was Fred, calling from the direction of the car.

"We're coming, Fred."

"I've just shot someone," Fred said. He was gripping his pistol with both hands, pointing downward behind a mailbox.

Stone looked down and saw a bald head with its back missing and brains coming out. "Holy shit," he said, thrusting Holly at Fred. "Get her into the car, we're going to the hospital. I'll be right back."

Stone ran back to the entrance, shoved the door open, and yelled at a room full of cops and people in evening dress. "Gunshot, man down behind the mailbox. I'm going to Lenox Hill Hospital, meet me there." He ran back around the corner and jumped into the car. "Go, Fred!" He looked back as they drove away and saw a stream of cops pouring into the street.

"U-turn, then right on East Seventy-seventh Street!" he said to Fred, more quietly now. He pulled a fresh linen handkerchief from his inside pocket and pressed it against Holly's wound. "Hold this right there," he said, as the red traffic signals blew by and the sound of horns followed them. "And a happy new year to you, too," Stone muttered.

Fred made the turn on Seventy-seventh and screeched to a halt in front of the ER awning.

"You stay here for a second, and I'll be right back," Stone said to Holly. He leaped out of the car, ran around it, and barged into the building, where a pair of gurneys were in the hallway, and he grabbed one of them. "Gunshot wound in the street!" he yelled at a pair of nurses locked in conversation, then he rammed a gurney through the swinging doors and pushed it outside, where

Holly was on the sidewalk, leaning against the car, supported by Fred.

"I can walk," she said.

Stone picked her up bodily and laid her gently on the cart. "Entering on a gurney impresses them with the urgency," he said.

The two nurses got to the doors in time to open them, and Stone trotted the gurney into the building and headed for a door marked "Exam One." "A little help over here," he shouted at a young doctor stretched out on one of the two tables in the room.

The man vaulted off the table as Stone lifted Holly onto the other table.

"Oh, for God's sake," she said, "it's not all that bad."

The doctor, who wore a badge saying "Dr. Battle," peeled back the stole, pulled down one side of her dress, revealing a handsome breast, then pulled it back up and ran his hand over her shoulder. "She's right," he said. "Small caliber, bullet still lodged. I can feel it in her back."

A nurse came into the room. "Disposition, Doctor?"

"Surgery," he said. "Call Ted Barnes and tell him to get his ass over here and scrub. Gunshot wound to the left shoulder. Female, maybe forty, and quite beautiful.

That'll get him moving."

"Aren't you kind?" Holly said, as the doctor began pushing the table out of the exam room.

"I'm right behind you," Stone said, trotting along.

"You won't be necessary," the doctor said to him.

"I'm no more unnecessary pacing outside an operating room than I am down here," Stone said.

Holly was being wheeled into an elevator when two cops appeared and each took one of Stone's arms.

"I'm needed in surgery," he told the cops.

"The hell he is," the doctor said as the doors closed.

They sat Stone down on a bench next to Fred, who was reading a *New York Post* he had found there. "Disgusting," he said, casting the newspaper aside.

"Okay," a cop said, "who's shot?"

"The lady in the elevator," Stone replied. "She's on her way to surgery. Come see her tomorrow."

"We got a second victim back at Sixty-third and Park," the cop said. "Did he shoot the first victim?"

"Yes, sir," Fred replied, "and I shot him, but half a second too late." He removed his pistol from his shoulder holster, popped out the magazine, cleared the weapon, locked the slide open, and handed it to the nearest cop. "I expect you'll want this," he said.

Next through the door was Dino, at a trot. "What the fuck is going on here?" he demanded of everybody present.

They all began to talk at once, including a nurse who had been eavesdropping.

"You," Dino said, pointing at Stone. "Gimme a hint on what happened."

"Some guy in a motorcycle suit shot Holly. She's upstairs in surgery, looks like a .22 to the left shoulder, I'd say it missed the lung. Fred witnessed this and shot the shooter in the back of the head."

"Half a second too late," Fred said. "Yer man has got my gun."

The cop held it up for Dino to see.

Dino pointed at Fred. "That man is not under arrest," he said to the cop.

"Yessir."

"Process his weapon, get ballistics on it, and when it's all wrapped up, give Mr. Flicker here back his gun."

"Yessir."

Dino sat down next to Stone. "Okay," he said, "who's trying to kill you?"

"Me?" Stone asked, pointing at himself

with his thumb. "Who would want to kill me?"

"That's my line," Dino pointed out. "Who?"

"Nobody, that's who — I don't have an enemy in the world."

"Stone," Dino said, exasperated, "people try to kill you all the time. Not so long ago somebody tried to bomb your house, remember?"

"All my enemies are either dead or in jail."

"Anybody get out recently? I mean, apart from the fresh ex-con who tried to shoot you tonight? Through the miracle of modern technology, we managed to fingerprint the corpse without even giving him a ride to the morgue."

"And who is he?"

"One Vernon Percival Jackson, aka 'Crank' to his nearest and dearest cell mates, out of Fishkill six days ago and dying to meet you, so he could put a bullet in your head."

"Then he's very bad at his work, isn't he? Do I have to remind you that he shot our secretary of state?"

Across the room a nurse beat it to her station and made a phone call to a reporter she knew who paid for such services.

"So, he was distracted by Fred shooting him in the head," Dino said. "That kind of thing can put a guy's aim off."

"I did hear two shots, now that I recall," Stone said. "One little one and one big one."

"Which came first?"

"I'm not sure, they were very close together."

"Trust me, the big one came first and ruined Mr. Jackson's aim, as well as his day."

"Then who made the little bang?" Stone asked. "Wait a minute, I've just remembered something."

"Your words make a policeman's heart happy," Dino said.

"Fishkill — I know somebody who just got out of Fishkill."

"Who might that be, and how did you make his acquaintance?"

"I didn't, exactly. A guy named Alphonse Teppi . . ."

"I remember running that name for you."

"Right. He wanted me to get a friend of his named Danny Blaine out of Fishkill."

"Which you did not do, as I recall."

"You recall correctly. I pretty much threw Teppi out of my office."

"Now we have two people to investigate, just like that." Dino snapped his fingers.

"And I saw Teppi earlier this evening," Stone said.

"See? It's all coming back to you. Where?"

"At Studio 54. We were watching Michael Feinstein."

"I hope we don't have to bring Feinstein into this. I like his work."

"No, no, he was just singing. Teppi was listening."

"And he saw you?"

"Yes, and I think he made a phone call."

"Aha! A phone call! My blood is atingle," Dino said.

"Hey, something else," Stone said. "This guy was riding a motorcycle, right?"

"He was."

"Well, Joan said she spotted a thug on a motorcycle outside the house. She wanted to take a shot at him."

"Had she done so, she might have saved us all a lot of trouble," Dino said.

A reporter at the *Post,* screwing his girl-friend on a sofa, surrounded by toy hats and empty champagne bottles, stopped. His cell phone was ringing. "I gotta get this," he said to her.

"Don't mind me," she replied, closing her legs.

"Yeah?"

"Mickey, it's Peggy, at Lenox Hill."

"Make it quick, Peggy, I'm in a conference."

"Yeah, I'll bet, on New Year's Eve."

"I said quick!"

"We got the secretary of state in here with a gunshot wound."

"The secretary of what?"

"State, that Holly lady."

"Barker?"

"That's the one."

"Who shot her?"

"I don't know, but there's cops everywhere. The lady's in surgery — small-caliber gunshot wound, left shoulder, up high. I saw the wound myself, before they took her upstairs."

Mickey leaped to his feet, tripping over his pants, which were around his ankles. "I'm on my way, baby, and you're getting champagne for this."

"I'd prefer cash," she said, and hung up.

"Mickey," his girlfriend said, helping him up. "Are we screwing or what?"

"Later, babe," he said, adjusting his clothing and buckling his belt. "Big story afoot."

367

He grabbed his coat and hat and ran for the door.

"Don't wake me up when you get home!" she shouted after him.

# 58

Stone's head had fallen forward as he sat in the waiting room, and he was dozing when a man burst through the double doors of the ER.

"Where is she?" he shouted.

"Where's who?" Dino asked.

"That Holly . . . Whatshername."

"You're drunk," Dino said. "Get out of here."

"Only a little drunk," the man said. "It's New Year's Eve, after all."

Dino looked at the uniformed cop standing there and made a little motion with his head.

The cop took the man by the wrist and elbow and frog-marched him out onto the street, then returned. "Taken care of, Commish," he said to Dino.

The man outside crashed through the doors again. "Didn't you ever hear of freedom of the press?"

"Didn't you ever hear of getting your head broken?" the cop asked.

"You hear that, Commissioner?" he shouted. "I'm Mickey Fields from the *Post.*"

"What do you want?" Dino asked.

"Where's the secretary of state?"

"Try Washington, D.C."

A nurse who was leaning on the opposite wall, her arms akimbo, caught the reporter's eye and pointed up with a thumb.

"Never mind," Fields said, then ran for the elevator. He was on his way upstairs before the cop could reach him.

"Is there a uniform upstairs?" Dino asked the cop.

"Yessir."

"Radio him that a maniac is on the way up and to stop him."

The cop made the call.

A man with a camera hung around his neck ran in. "Where's Mickey Fields?" he asked.

"Under arrest," Dino replied. "You want to join him?"

"You can't arrest Mickey Fields, Commissioner," the man said.

"I can arrest anybody who's causing a disturbance," Dino replied.

"Who's causing a disturbance?"

"You are."

Before a cop could throw him out, the elevator doors opened and Dr. Battle walked out, followed closely by Mickey Fields. "She's out of surgery and in recovery," the doctor said. "We'll keep her overnight and discharge her in the morning."

"That's who I'm looking for," the photographer said, pointing at Fields.

"Nobody can see her," the doctor said. "She's in recovery."

Stone got up, walked to the elevator, and got on. Fields and the photographer tried to follow him in, but he lifted a leg and kicked them both out. The doors closed.

"Commissioner," Fields said, "I want to file charges against that guy!"

"Go fuck yourself," Dino said.

Stone found the recovery room and, inside, Holly on a gurney, eyes closed. A nurse stood by.

"You can't come in here," the nurse said.

"Yes, he can," Holly said, suddenly awake. "You shut up."

The nurse looked outraged, but she shut up.

Stone leaned over her and kissed her on the forehead.

"First time you've ever kissed me there," she said.

"What do you need?" Stone asked. "Anything at all?"

"Get me a change of clothes and come back in the morning," she said. "I need a good night's sleep." She closed her eyes again.

Fred drove Stone home. "Mr. Barrington, I'm sorry I had to shoot that bloke," he said.

"You did the right thing, Fred, don't worry about it."

"How's Madam Secretary?"

"Pleasantly medicated and asleep," Stone replied. "We'll go back to the hospital first thing in the morning."

Once home, Stone went upstairs, hung up his dinner jacket, and fell into bed.

Stone had breakfast while watching the morning news; Holly was all over it — the attempt on the life of the secretary of state. Everybody on TV was going nuts — people reporting from outside Lenox Hill's ER, cameras everywhere.

"Drive around the block," Stone said to Fred. "Let's find another entrance." He picked up some flowers from a market on the way.

Holly was sitting up in bed, her left arm in

a sling, eating scrambled eggs. He kissed her. "How are you doing?" he asked.

"I'm ravenous," she said, stuffing bacon into her mouth and taking a bite out of a bagel.

He held up a small bag. "Change of clothes, makeup, et cetera."

"Good boy." She shoved her empty plate aside and swung her legs over the side of the bed.

A doctor walked in. "Whoa," he said, "are you up to that?"

Holly stood up. "I'm just fine, and I'm going . . . home," she replied, picking up her bag and walking toward the bathroom. "I won't be a minute," she said to Stone, kissing him. She closed the door behind her.

"How is she?" Stone said.

"She looks okay to me," the doctor replied.

"Don't you have to examine her?"

"I did that before she had breakfast. She was raring to go. You want to argue with her?"

"No," Stone replied.

A Secret Service agent knocked at the open door and came into the room.

"Good morning, Agent," Stone said.

"I hear you got my boss shot last night," the man said.

"That's a dirty communist lie," Stone said.

A nurse came in with a plastic shopping bag and handed it to the doctor, who handed it to Stone.

"Change her bandage daily," he said. "She's had an antibiotic injection, and there are pills in the bag. At the slightest sign of infection, get her back here. Her stitches will come out in ten days."

"Will she have a scar?" Stone asked. "She'll worry about that."

"We had a plastic surgeon close her incisions, front and back, and they're small, so that shouldn't be an issue. He offered to come and see her, if it will make her feel better." He handed Stone two cards. "Him and me," he said, then left.

Holly came out, looking fresh. "Thanks for the hairbrush," she said to Stone. They got her into a wheelchair and rolled her onto an elevator and out the back door. Stone waved at Fred, who was parked by the door, and he pulled up and opened a door for her. The agent followed in the usual black SUV.

"What are the media saying?" Holly asked.

"You're feisty, hardy, and brave," Stone replied.

"I'll settle for that," she said.

# 59

Gloria Parsons was scrambling eggs at midmorning, while Benton slept in for an extra half hour. Her cell phone buzzed, and she answered it.

"Ms. Parsons?"

"Yes."

"It's Benny, the super, downtown."

"Hi, Benny. Anything wrong down there?"

"I'm not sure. There were two cops, detectives, here, but I told them you were away, and they left."

"You did good, Benny. Thanks for calling." She hung up with a sick feeling in her stomach.

They were having breakfast in bed when the doorman rang from downstairs and Benton answered. "Yes? . . . What do they want? . . . Oh, all right, send them up."

"What's going on?" Gloria asked.

"How the hell do I know? There are two detectives on the way up."

Gloria put on a robe over her naked body and cleared away the dishes.

Benton came into the kitchen. "They want to talk to you," he said.

"Me?"

Benton walked out, and the two detectives walked in, waving badges.

"What can I do for you?" Gloria asked, continuing to load the dishwasher.

"Ms. Parsons, are you acquainted with a Danny Blaine?"

"Yes."

"How about an Alphonse Teppi?"

"Yes, I know them both."

"How about a bald guy named Jackson, nickname Crank."

"I don't know him, never heard of him."

"Did you receive a phone call from Mr. Teppi about nine forty-five last evening?"

"He left a message, but I deleted it."

"Why?"

"I didn't want to talk to him. I was at a party — at the police commissioner's home."

"Did you receive a call yesterday from Mr. Blaine?"

"Yes, and I sent it directly to voice mail."

"Why?

"I didn't want to talk to him. I'm tired of both those characters. They used to phone me with tips that I could write about, but I'm not in that business anymore, and I don't need them."

"Ms. Parsons, we'd like to take a look at your cell phone. May we borrow it for a couple of hours?"

"You may not, unless you have a search warrant. I'm a journalist, and I have a right to privacy."

"As you wish," the man said, and they both left.

Benton came back into the kitchen. "What was that about?"

"They asked me about some phone calls I received but didn't answer. They were from people I don't want to know anymore."

"Okay," he said.

She got dressed, walked over to the Apple store, and bought the latest iPhone, then called Teppi on the old one. She left a message. "Don't call me for a year, and tell Danny not to either." She had them scrub the old phone of data, then activate a new number, then she did some shopping in the neighborhood and went back to Benton's apartment.

Stone and Holly were having lunch in the kitchen when Dino called.

"Hey."

"Happy new year," Dino said.

"Didn't we cover that last night?"

"There's stuff we didn't cover last night."

"Tell me."

"We took a throwaway cell phone off the dead guy from last night. Guess who called him a couple of hours before he met his maker?"

"I give up."

"Danny Blaine."

"That's weird. What does it mean?"

"We brought Blaine in and went through his cell phone. He had a call from Alphonse Teppi around the same time you saw him at Studio 54."

"Uh-oh."

"And get this — Danny Blaine and the shooter were neighbors at Fishkill. Blaine bought protection from the guy Jackson, known as 'Crank.' "

"I think I'm getting the picture — both of them are friends of Gloria Parsons."

"I've got two detectives getting a search warrant for her phone right now. She refused to give it to them earlier."

"So this was about me, not Holly?"

"What did I say to you last night?"

"Let me know what you find on her phone."

"I'll get back to you." Dino hung up.

■ ■ ■ ■

When Gloria got home the two detectives were sitting in the living room with Benton, drinking coffee. This surprised her, because she didn't know that Benton knew how to make coffee.

"Give them your cell phone," Benton said, holding up a sheet of paper. "They've got a warrant."

The detectives received the phone, then stood up. "We'll bring it back later."

"Wait a minute," Benton said, holding up a single finger. He looked over the warrant. "This gives you the right to search it, not confiscate it."

"Okay, my partner can do what we need."

His partner began going over the phone. "There's nothing here," he said after a couple of minutes. "It's been scrubbed clean."

"It's new," Gloria said.

"When did you buy it?"

"What is this about?" Gloria asked. "Tell me, and I'll tell you if I know anything."

"Gentlemen?" Benton said. "Ask your questions."

"All right. When did you last see Alphonse Teppi and Danny Blaine?"

"It's been several weeks," she replied, "maybe months. The governor and I went to Bermuda for a week."

"Right," Benton said.

"Then I was on assignment in the Florida Keys for a week after that."

"And before that?"

"I don't remember the last time I saw either of them," Gloria said. "These are the sort of people I would run into now and then when I was writing gossip-based stuff, but they weren't really friends. I don't do that kind of work anymore."

"Governor," a detective said, "why did you commute Danny Blaine's prison sentence?"

"Because I asked him to," Gloria said quickly. "I felt sorry for the kid. He was being abused in prison."

"Actually, he wasn't being abused," the cop said. "He was buying protection from a fellow inmate."

"He wrote me a letter saying he was being abused," she said. "I didn't ask for details, and I don't know who his friends were in prison."

"I can help you out there — he was buying protection from Crank Jackson."

"Who the hell is that?" she asked.

"He's the man who shot the secretary of state on New Year's Eve. You were there, remember?"

"Of course I remember," she said, "but I don't know this man."

"Are you trying to tie Ms. Parsons to the shooting?" Benton asked.

"We're investigating the shooter."

"Well, Ms. Parsons was with me at a party at the police commissioner's apartment, and I can tell you, she had nothing to do with a shooting."

"What would I have against the secretary of state?" Gloria asked. "I admire her. I wrote a complimentary magazine piece about her."

"I think that'll do it, gentlemen," Benton said. "You're obviously on the wrong track, here."

"Thank you, Governor, Ms. Parsons," the man said, and they gave Gloria back her phone and left.

"Gloria," Benton said when they had gone, "why did you get a new cell phone?"

"I had all sorts of stuff on my old phone — notes for pieces, people I'd interviewed, lots of stuff," she said. "I didn't want them pawing through all of that."

"Okay," he said. "I just wondered."

"Sweetie," she said, putting her hand on his crotch, "I am not part of a conspiracy to murder the secretary of state. The whole business is preposterous."

"You're right," Benton said, as she unzipped his fly.

# 60

Stone was watching Holly get dressed for her speech at the UN, and she was using her wounded shoulder, though gingerly. "It's good that you're moving that," he said.

"I know."

"What's your speech about at the UN?" he asked her.

"Middle East terrorism. I've spoken to the Security Council once before, but this is my first speech to the General Assembly."

The phone rang, and Stone didn't wait for Joan to pick it up. "Hello?"

"It's Dino."

"Good morning."

"Okay," Dino said, "here's where we are. We can connect Alphonse Teppi and Danny Blaine through cell phone calls on the night, and Parsons received a call from each but says she sent them to voice mail, but Teppi and Blaine were using throwaways, and they had only one connected call each. We can connect Crank Jackson with Danny, but only with one call. Parsons used Teppi and Blaine as informants for magazine pieces, but we can't put her together with them for weeks. She says she no longer needs their services and doesn't want to know them."

"So?"

"So, we've got a glimmer of a case, but no grounds for arrest and no chance of a conviction based on the available evidence. And it's my people's considered judgment that we're not going to get any further. Frankly, we've no motive for Gloria Parsons wanting you dead. It's my guess that she may have said something offhand about knocking you off, and they may have taken it seriously. As far as we can tell, she harbors no ill feelings toward you."

"So, everybody walks?"

"Everybody but Crank Jackson. He's not going anywhere but to potter's field."

"Okay, I buy that. I think you got it right."

"If I'm wrong, we'll hear from some of them again, but I don't think that's going to happen. They know how close we came to nailing them. If we'd landed Jackson and turned him, they'd all be on Rikers Island right now."

"Tell you what I'm going to do," Stone

said. "I'm going to put it all right out of my mind."

"I'm happy for you. See ya." Dino hung up.

Stone turned back to Holly; she was dressed and ready to go, and she was wearing an Hermès silk scarf as a sling for her arm. "Changed your mind, huh?"

"It's a look," she said.

On the way to the UN he told her about Dino's call. "Looks like they were after me all along," he said. "You've nothing to worry about."

"Do me a favor," she said. "Don't say a word about that to anybody."

Stone laughed. "My lips are sealed."

They were met at the front door of the building by a UN official, who escorted them to the General Assembly hall. Stone was escorted to a seat in the VIP gallery while Holly waited in the wings.

The president of the General Assembly introduced her, and she walked to the podium. Applause became a roar when they saw her arm in the sling. The audience of diplomats — even the Russians and Chinese

— stood and cheered for a good two minutes.

Finally, Holly quieted them. She opened the notebook containing the speech, looked for the Teleprompter screens, and began to speak.

# AUTHOR'S NOTE

I am happy to hear from readers, but you should know that if you write to me in care of my publisher, three to six months will pass before I receive your letter, and when it finally arrives it will be one among many, and I will not be able to reply.

However, if you have access to the Internet, you may visit my website at www.stuartwoods.com, where there is a button for sending me e-mail. So far, I have been able to reply to all my e-mail, and I will continue to try to do so.

If you send me an e-mail and do not receive a reply, it is probably because you are among an alarming number of people who have entered their e-mail address incorrectly in their mail software. I have many of my replies returned as undeliverable.

Remember: e-mail, reply; snail mail, no reply.

When you e-mail, please do not send attachments, as I never open these. They can take twenty minutes to download, and they often contain viruses.

Please do not place me on your mailing lists for funny stories, prayers, political causes, charitable fund-raising, petitions, or sentimental claptrap. I get enough of that from people I already know. Generally speaking, when I get e-mail addressed to a large number of people, I immediately delete it without reading it.

Please do not send me your ideas for a book, as I have a policy of writing only what I myself invent. If you send me story ideas, I will immediately delete them without reading them. If you have a good idea for a book, write it yourself, but I will not be able to advise you on how to get it published. Buy a copy of *Writer's Market* at any bookstore; that will tell you how.

Anyone with a request concerning events or appearances may e-mail it to me or send it to: Publicity Department, Penguin Random House LLC, 375 Hudson Street, New York, NY 10014.

Those ambitious folk who wish to buy film, dramatic, or television rights to my books should contact Matthew Snyder, Creative Artists Agency, 9830 Wilshire Boulevard, Beverly Hills, CA 98212-1825.

Those who wish to make offers for rights of a literary nature should contact Anne Sibbald, Janklow & Nesbit, 445 Park Avenue, New York, NY 10022. (Note: This is not an invitation for you to send her your manuscript or to solicit her to be your agent.)

If you want to know if I will be signing books in your city, please visit my website, www.stuartwoods.com, where the tour schedule will be published a month or so in advance. If you wish me to do a book signing in your locality, ask your favorite bookseller to contact his Penguin representative or the Penguin publicity department with the request.

If you find typographical or editorial errors in my book and feel an irresistible urge to tell someone, please write to Sara Minnich at Penguin's address above. Do not e-mail your discoveries to me, as I will already have learned about them from others.

A list of my published works appears on my website. All the novels are still in print in paperback and can be found at or ordered from any bookstore. If you wish to obtain hardcover copies of earlier novels or of the two nonfiction books, a good used-book store or one of the online bookstores can help you find them. Otherwise, you will have to go to a great many garage sales.

# ABOUT THE AUTHOR

**Stuart Woods** is the author of more than sixty novels, including the *New York Times*–bestselling Stone Barrington and Holly Barker series. He is a native of Georgia and began his writing career in the advertising industry. *Chiefs*, his debut in 1981, won the Edgar Award. An avid sailor and pilot, Woods lives in New York City, Florida, and Maine.

F. W. H.